IF SHE FEARED

A JESSIE HUNT PSYCHOLOGICAL SUSPENSE SERIES
THE PERFECT WIFE (Book #1)
THE PERFECT BLOCK (Book #2)
THE PERFECT HOUSE (Book #3)
THE PERFECT SMILE (Book #4)
THE PERFECT LIE (Book #5)

CHLOE FINE PSYCHOLOGICAL SUSPENSE SERIES
NEXT DOOR (Book #1)
A NEIGHBOR'S LIE (Book #2)
CUL DE SAC (Book #3)
SILENT NEIGHBOR (Book #4)
HOMECOMING (Book #5)
TINTED WINDOWS (Book #6)

KATE WISE MYSTERY SERIES
IF SHE KNEW (Book #1)
IF SHE SAW (Book #2)
IF SHE RAN (Book #3)
IF SHE HID (Book #4)
IF SHE FLED (Book #5)
IF SHE FEARED (Book #6)
IF SHE HEARD (Book #7)

THE MAKING OF RILEY PAIGE SERIES
WATCHING (Book #1)
WAITING (Book #2)
LURING (Book #3)

TAKING (Book #4)
STALKING (Book #5)

RILEY PAIGE MYSTERY SERIES
ONCE GONE (Book #1)
ONCE TAKEN (Book #2)
ONCE CRAVED (Book #3)
ONCE LURED (Book #4)
ONCE HUNTED (Book #5)
ONCE PINED (Book #6)
ONCE FORSAKEN (Book #7)
ONCE COLD (Book #8)
ONCE STALKED (Book #9)
ONCE LOST (Book #10)
ONCE BURIED (Book #11)
ONCE BOUND (Book #12)
ONCE TRAPPED (Book #13)
ONCE DORMANT (Book #14)
ONCE SHUNNED (Book #15)
ONCE MISSED (Book #16)

MACKENZIE WHITE MYSTERY SERIES
BEFORE HE KILLS (Book #1)
BEFORE HE SEES (Book #2)
BEFORE HE COVETS (Book #3)
BEFORE HE TAKES (Book #4)
BEFORE HE NEEDS (Book #5)
BEFORE HE FEELS (Book #6)
BEFORE HE SINS (Book #7)
BEFORE HE HUNTS (Book #8)
BEFORE HE PREYS (Book #9)
BEFORE HE LONGS (Book #10)
BEFORE HE LAPSES (Book #11)
BEFORE HE ENVIES (Book #12)
BEFORE HE STALKS (Book #13)

IF SHE FEARED

A Kate Wise Mystery—Book 6

BLAKE PIERCE

BLAKE PIERCE

Blake Pierce is author of the bestselling RILEY PAGE mystery series, which includes fifteen books (and counting). Blake Pierce is also the author of the MACKENZIE WHITE mystery series, comprising thirteen books (and counting); of the AVERY BLACK mystery series, comprising six books; of the KERI LOCKE mystery series, comprising five books; of the MAKING OF RILEY PAIGE mystery series, comprising four books (and counting); of the KATE WISE mystery series, comprising six books (and counting); of the CHLOE FINE psychological suspense mystery, comprising five books (and counting); and of the JESSE HUNT psychological suspense thriller series, comprising five books (and counting).

ONCE GONE (a Riley Paige Mystery—Book #1), BEFORE HE KILLS (A Mackenzie White Mystery—Book 1), CAUSE TO KILL (An Avery Black Mystery—Book 1), A TRACE OF DEATH (A Keri Locke Mystery—Book 1), and WATCHING (The Making of Riley Paige—Book 1) are each available as a free download on Amazon!

An avid reader and lifelong fan of the mystery and thriller genres, Blake loves to hear from you, so please feel free to visit www.blakepierceauthor.com to learn more and stay in touch.

TABLE OF CONTENTS

PROLOGUE

When Tamara Bateman walked into the two-story house at 3:30 in the afternoon, she was reminded of why she loved her job so much. As a real estate agent in Estes, Delaware, she saw at least four new houses a week. Most of the time, those homes were so-so at best—carbon copies of other homes in the area, usually with a price tag somewhere in the upper four hundred thousands. But every now and then she'd step into a house and get a sort of tingle…a feeling that this house was going to make an exceptional home for someone.

The house at 157 Hammermill Street was one of those homes. It wasn't a brand new build like some of the houses she had shown this week, but it was new enough. Built in 2005, and only lived in by a married couple with no kids before being sold to a property owner who fixed it up even more, it still had that new-home smell. Of course, that had a lot to do with the immaculate cleaning job the hired cleaners had done.

It was a gorgeous house. All of the floors had been polished, there was a fresh coat of paint on every wall, and the picture windows that looked out onto the garden in the backyard were to die for. With the touch of a professional stager and some modern furniture, the place would go quickly and make a great home.

Tamara had been showing it for two weeks now, and while there was some general interest, there had not yet been a legitimate offer. With no furniture and having recently been cleaned spotless, it was essentially a blank canvas. But she was also starting to wonder if the lack of furnishings was what was hurting it.

1

She took out her phone and started taking notes, trying to improve the public listing. She knew there was no real science to writing the copy on the sell sheets, but she enjoyed doing it. She felt she had a knack for it—almost as if she was a weird sort of poet. And since she had two showings tomorrow, she wanted to make sure she was presenting it in its best light.

She walked through the large living space, then the gorgeous kitchen with its farmhouse sink and industrial-looking barstools. As she was trying to come up with a non-mundane word for the marble countertops, she heard something move upstairs. It was just a slight shuffling, barely there at all but definitely there. She cocked her head and listened for the noise again, and sure enough, there it was.

The noise was not footsteps, but softer. She imagined one of the windows opened, the light autumn breeze outside blowing the curtains. That was almost *exactly* what it sounded like. But she didn't think anyone had been in here for two or three days. And the only people who had keys to the place right now were herself and the contractor.

She almost decided to ignore it, but then it came again. This time she was almost certain the sound was the rustling of curtains. But she could not see the contractor coming through and opening a window—much less opening it and leaving it open.

She instantly tried to recall if it had rained in the past three days. She didn't think so, but even if not, there were all kinds of birds and insects that could fly in. Irritated, Tamara marched back through the living area and to the staircase that led to the second floor. As she climbed the steps, she rolled through phrases in her head to explain how wide and spacious the stairs were.

Before she reached the top of the stairs, she heard the noise again. This time it was louder and more constant. And now she wasn't so sure it was the shuffling of curtains. Now, it *did* sound like footsteps.

But that made no sense. Only the owner and the contractor—a fifty-six-year-old man named Bob—had the other key and he was in New York right now, enjoying a show with his wife. Tamara knew this because he had griped about it the last time they'd seen one another. And the owner never bothered with any of his houses once they were listed by the real estate agency.

So who the hell is up there?

She surprised herself when she took a few more steps up. She was only two stairs shy of the second-floor hallway. She could see the carpet and the bottoms of the first two opened doors along the hall.

She nearly called out, but thought that would be stupid. If there *was* someone here, maybe it would benefit her for them to not know she was there.

Don't be stupid, she told herself. *There's nothing in this house to steal. If there is anyone here, it's either Bob or some nosy neighbor. And if they got in, it means the contractor left the door unlocked like an idiot. It wouldn't be the first time Bob forgot to lock up a property after stopping by.*

But then the footsteps came again, from somewhere very close. And then there was the sound of breathing—anxious, excited breathing.

Tamara then followed her instincts. She fought off her curiosity and bolted down the stairs. She fumbled with her phone, intending to call the police. Even if it did turn out to be nothing, she'd rather be safe than sorry. She'd rather—

She heard footsteps thundering behind her. She felt the tremors in the stairway beneath her feet. She let out a little scream as she neared the bottom of the stairs, but it never had time to fully come out of her mouth. Something struck her hard from behind, connecting solidly with the back of her head and her upper back.

Tamara went sprawling toward the floor. She threw her hands up to keep from smashing her face. In doing so, she twisted her wrist. She heard it snap but was only dimly aware of it. She was still thinking of those thundering footsteps that had come from behind her. She was in a foggy daze, her head screaming in pain and her wrist starting to throb in a dull ache. She tried to turn to see her attacker but never got the chance.

She felt something rough slide over her head and then rest on her neck. It was then drawn tight ... and suddenly she was no longer fighting to turn over to face her attacker.

She was now fighting to breathe.

And as the darkness came in, the pain in her head overwhelmed by the desperate pain in her neck and lungs, it was a fight she lost quickly.

CHAPTER ONE

The kids on *Stranger Things* were starting to annoy Kate Wise. She supposed it made sense. They were just like any other kids. Exciting and cute when you first met them, but with a tendency to get irritating as they got older. Kate felt she knew the *Stranger Things* kids pretty well; she had binged seasons one and two over the course of three days. And now that she was staring season three in the face, she didn't think she had it in her.

Kate set her Apple TV remote down on her coffee table and stood up. She looked at the clock and was a bit disgusted to find that it had somehow come to be 5:10 in the afternoon. She then looked at the end table by the couch, at the stack of books she had purchased from the used book store in Carytown last weekend. She'd started one—a rather dull look at the life of John Wayne Gacy—but had not had the mental capacity to handle it ... or any book, for that matter.

So she'd taken to finally using her Netflix account, something she only had because Allen had talked her into it. They had watched a few things together, mostly documentaries and *The Office*, but had quickly discovered that when they were together, they much preferred to talk. But when Kate was alone as of late, she found that she preferred to just veg out. She'd never really enjoyed spending a lot of time in front of the television but lately, it seemed she was starting to enjoy mindless things that just let her unplug and detach from everything. She was beginning to enjoy the idea of escaping the real world; whether it was spending some time with the kids in the Upside Down or trying to feign interest in *Grey's Anatomy*, it was nice to mentally check out and view someone else's drama for a while.

She'd had plenty of time to do it, after all. Director Duran had stayed true to his angry words and had not reached out to her in over six weeks. She knew she was not fired, but that she was only being considered for cases needing her expert touch or in-depth research. He had scolded her a bit and then told her she'd only be used in a research capacity—a lifeline for other agents at most. She understood it; she was a bit too careless for her age when she was on the job, as evidenced by the last case. But he also knew she was good at what she did and was not ready to have her removed just yet.

So far, none of that had come about. As she had waited for his call, her life had gone on. In those stagnant six weeks, she had turned fifty-six, her granddaughter, Michelle, had turned one year old, and she and Allen had gone on two trips—one to a remote cabin in the Blue Ridge Mountains and another to Surfside Beach, South Carolina, to get one last hoorah out of the summer.

But that last trip had been two weeks ago. When they had come back, Allen had returned to work. While he still had his own place, he spent most of his time at Kate's house. They had discussed permanently moving in together and she supposed that's where they were headed. She thought about those sorts of things while wasting her days away. But then she'd found *Stranger Things* and, God help her, *Grey's Anatomy*, and had plenty of ways to fill those long expanses of empty time.

She'd tinkered with writing the book she'd always wanted to write—a look at some of her more bizarre cases. She had about fifty pages down, but all that had done was remind her that her glory days were now behind her. Even with an agent already interested (though it was really just one of those friend-of-a-friend type of deals), she could not find the motivation to get the book moving along.

She knew she was in a rut. If Duran had decided he no longer needed her anymore, she really wished he'd just say something.

Being let go, she thought, would be preferable to being left in the dark.

She had another hour before Allen would be home. With the TV finally off, she thought about the book but knew she didn't have the drive to work on it today. She looked to her cell phone and thumbed through her old texts. She had received one from Kristen DeMarco five days ago, just checking in. She was still active, filling in on cases with agents who, for some reason or another, were short a partner. Still, DeMarco had stayed in touch—a gesture Kate appreciated more than DeMarco would ever know.

DeMarco had become a friend very quickly. This was saying a lot, as Kate had always been very good about drawing that thick line between partner and friend. But there was something about DeMarco that was different from all of her other partners. It was more than her promising career and her never-say-die charisma. She was a well-rounded woman who reminded Kate far too much of her younger self at times. And staying in touch with her had been one of the more pivotal cornerstones in Kate's life over the past six weeks.

Smiling, she pulled up DeMarco's number and called. She was not too surprised when it went to voice mail after four rings. She didn't bother leaving a message; DeMarco was probably working a case and while Kate did miss her, she did not want to interfere with her work.

She put the phone down and made her way into the kitchen. She and Allen had made plans to go out for dinner, so she wasn't going to have to cook. She leaned against the kitchen counter and looked through the window, out onto her backyard.

She supposed this was what an actual retirement might look like. Yes, she had experienced it a bit about a year and a half ago, but she had been *expecting* that one. She had busied herself with little hobbies and the occasional trip to the gun range. But this time, she felt bored and out of place. Maybe it was because she knew Duran could call at any moment and she'd be back into the flow of things.

Or maybe, she thought, it was some sort of foreshadowing—of the universe or God or something similar telling her that this would be her life soon. So she'd better strap herself in for the ride and get used to it.

They'd agreed on Thai food, which Kate was fine with because it had become one of her favorite types of food over the last few years. It was the same restaurant they frequented at least twice a month. As they were seated, Kate felt the familiarity of the place and wondered if this was another aspect of the retired (or, in her case, partially retired) life—becoming all too familiar with local eateries and businesses, stuck in a loop that felt as if there was no real purpose.

The monotony of the restaurant was broken by the topic of dinner conversation, though. Allen was retiring from his job as an advertising executive in three months. He would be leaving in two days to fly out to Chicago for a week or so and it would likely be his last trip before his retirement. His company was making a huge deal out of it and it had made Allen quite happy these last few days.

"They're saying I can bring a guest," Allen said as he dug into his dinner. "And they'll pay. So, if you want to spend a few days in Chicago with me…"

"That would be great," Kate said.

"I've noticed you being a little … I don't know … *distant*. Not in a bad way. You just seem bored. Lingering…"

"That's an accurate description," Kate said. "I thought I was hiding it better, though."

"Nope, not at all," Allen said with a smile. "Now, if you go with me, I'm going to be working a lot of the time. I trust you'll be fine by yourself, taking in the sights and doing some shopping in the Windy City."

"Yes, I think I'll be able to handle myself."

The flow of conversation between the two of them was natural. It had been nearly a year since they had started dating, and nearly five months since things had gotten very serious. They had not discussed marriage and had barely touched on the topic of actually living together—and that was fine with Kate. A large part of her heart was still reserved for her late husband, Michael. Whenever she tried to envision living the rest of her life with Allen, memories of Michael would surface and she didn't know if she was ready just yet.

"Have you talked to Melissa lately?" Allen asked.

"Yesterday. She called to let me know Michelle is almost walking. Not quite yet, but almost there…"

"Scary stuff," Allen said. "Once they start walking…"

"Oh, I know. Melissa was a holy terror once she was able to get her feet going. I remember one time when she—"

Her phone rang within her purse, interrupting her. She reached for it, assuming it was Melissa, as if summoned by the mention of her name. With a second thought, she ignored it. If it was Melissa, she'd leave a message and Kate would call her back later.

They carried on with dinner, reminiscing over the two recent trips they had taken. Kate noticed the way Allen had been looking at her lately. There was depth there, a sense of Allen almost sizing her up. It was a conceited thought, but she wondered if marriage was on his mind. At their age, spending so much time together didn't necessarily mean marriage was imminent, but every day that passed by had to count for something. She had no idea how she would react if he crossed that line, but it was still nice to think about.

Dinner came to an end, the check was delivered, and Allen quickly scooped it up. He knew she was not at all in any sort of financial distress; in fact, when she had retired the first time, she'd been looking at a comfortable retirement account to spend the rest of her life rather comfortably with. But Allen was all about making her feel secure when he could, like they were an actual dating couple. And to him, that meant the man had to pay.

"I'll catch up," Kate said as he stood up from his seat with the check in hand. "I think Melissa called while we were eating. I'd like to go ahead and call her back."

"Tell her I said hi," Allen said as he headed for the front of the restaurant.

Kate dug her phone out of her purse and saw that the missed call had not been from Melissa. It had been from Duran.

Excitement and guilt tore through her. She knew Duran would only call—at this hour, no less—for one reason. And if her gut was right (and it usually was), his reason for calling was likely going to mean that she could forget about the trip to Chicago with Allen.

No sense in wondering, she thought.

She returned the call right away, knowing that Duran was not the type to stay on the phone for very long. It rang only once before he answered.

"Kate, how are you?"

"Good." She knew that his use of her first name meant that he was in a hurry—that he wasn't going to be bothered by formalities.

"If you want in on it, I have a case for you. There shouldn't be too much heavy lifting, nothing too out of the ordinary."

"Well, of course I want it. What details do you have?"

"It's in Delaware. Two murders so far, very likely linked. I'd need you out there tomorrow. As for the specifics, I'll let the agent in charge of the case fill you in."

"Who is the agent?"

"DeMarco," Duran said. There seemed to be a bit of joy in his voice to reveal this. Even he could see the blossoming partnership the two had managed to grow. "She's handled things wonderfully so far, but it's starting to go nowhere fast, and she needs a hand. Of course, she won't admit it."

"Does she know I'm coming?"

"I'm going to call her when we get off of here to let her know. You mind driving? The bureau will comp you for gas."

"That sounds great." And while it really *did* sound great, she couldn't help but think of Allen and Chicago.

"Great. I'll call DeMarco and have her check in with me when you get there. Thanks, Wise."

He ended the call, leaving Kate to sit at the table for a moment to get her emotions sorted out. As she got to her feet, she spotted Allen waiting for her by the front door. There was a thin smile on his face as she approached him.

"That wasn't Melissa, was it?" he asked.

"How did you know?"

"You're very relaxed when you speak to her. The conversation you just had … it lit your face up. You were sitting perfectly upright, focusing very hard. It was Duran, wasn't it?"

"It was."

He nodded as he opened the door for her. When they were back on the street, bathed in the glow of the streetlights, he took her hand. "I'm going to assume Chicago is out?"

"I was presented an opportunity," she said. "I figured we could talk about it tonight."

"A case?"

"Yeah," she said.

"When would you be leaving?"

"Early tomorrow morning."

"Nothing to talk about then," he said. "Kate, we've been through this. I know how much that job means to you. So just go. Hell, I've got the work trip anyway. It would have been nice to have you there, sure, but we would have barely seen one another."

"Allen, I can—"

"It's okay. You know … I gave you an ultimatum several weeks ago. I still stand by it but this … I think it's okay. I do think we need to keep it in mind for when I finally kiss the working world goodbye."

"Three months," she said with a grin.

"I know. It's hard to believe."

The Thai place was only a mile and a half away from her house and they had chosen to walk—something they tried to do at least twice a week. The evening was nice, starting to chill a bit as the night crept in.

"So, if I leave around four thirty in the morning, you aren't going to get upset?" she asked a few moments later.

"No. I want you to enjoy this job while we can both withstand it. I won't be all that upset. Just make sure to kiss me before you go."

She leaned into him, wondering how she had ever managed to find a man as forgiving and understanding as Allen. And, with that, she also wondered how much longer he was going to put up with her sort-of job.

"If you keep up this understanding vibe you've got going on," she said, "you'll get a lot more than a kiss."

He laughed, wrapped his arm around her waist, and they continued on into the night.

CHAPTER TWO

It had been forever since Kate had driven through the early morning hours. She was out of the maze of DC exits and roadways by 4:50, heading northeast toward Delaware. She had checked her email the night before and had found nothing from Duran. But shortly after her alarm had gone off, she'd checked again and found, without much surprise, that Duran had sent her a specific location as well as electronic copies of the case files shortly after midnight.

The town the murders had occurred in was called Estes, a small town situated around Fallows Lake. Graced with the sunrise along the way, it made her think of the beach vacation she and Allen had taken; they'd spent one morning early on the beach, eating bagels and strawberries while watching the sunrise. While a lakeside town was a far stretch from a beach vacation, she imagined it still likely held some of the same charms... especially in the seasonal limbo that sat in those few weeks between the last true days of summer and the first cool days of fall.

The memory made her feel warm but also guilty. Allen had seemed almost *too* understanding about this sudden case. It made her wonder if he would reinforce his ultimatum three months from now, after he retired. He'd have a right to, she supposed. And that meant she had some serious things to think about.

For now, though, there was the case. And if the last case had taught her anything, it was that she was going to absolutely *have to* separate her personal life from her professional life. In some respects, it was even harder now than it had been when she'd been married and had a growing and rather difficult child on her hands.

She entered the town of Estes at 7:40 that morning, twenty minutes ahead of when she was scheduled to meet DeMarco at the latest crime scene. While the town was about a mile away from the lake, Estes was built in a way that made it feel like you were right on the shore. Hell, there were certain features of the area that made it appear as if the *ocean* was just around the corner rather than a lake. The homes were all coastal in appearance and there were several gift shops along the main stretch that looked as if they had simply wandered away from the Delaware beaches that sat about eighty miles to the east. Being early, Kate swung by a small coffee shop and ordered a dark roast before heading for the latest crime scene.

When she arrived five minutes early, she found DeMarco already there. She was parked in the paved driveway, sipping her own coffee while leaning against what was clearly a bureau car. She smiled and waved at Kate as she parked next to her.

"Hey," Kate said as she stepped out. "Sorry to crash your party."

"I'll be honest," DeMarco said. "I was sort of happy when Duran called and told me he was sending you."

"Is the case running away from you a bit?" Kate asked.

"No, not really. But this was my first solo case and so far, there's nothing really popping, you know?" She looked up at the sky and smiled. "I know it's just a simple lake, but have you ever noticed how even the sky starts to look different the closer you get to open water?"

"No, I haven't," Kate said, looking skyward. She realized DeMarco was simply trying to avoid the fact that, when it was all boiled down, Duran had called Kate in because DeMarco had been unable to push the case forward on her own. She wondered how long DeMarco would be able to go without saying such a thing out loud.

"Did Duran send you the case files?" DeMarco asked as she started walking toward the house. It was a two-story mock beach house, another of the homes that would have looked right at home along the Delaware coast. There was a FOR SALE sign at the edge of the yard, adorned by a pretty woman's smiling face.

Her name—Tamara Bateman—and number were listed below her bright profile.

"He did, but I figured it would save me some time and headache if I just heard it straight from you."

"Seems simple enough," DeMarco said. "Two murders in Estes within a week of one another. The latest victim is that pretty lady right there." She nodded back toward the FOR SALE sign.

"When was she killed?"

"Two days ago. I was called in yesterday, got here a little later than I would have preferred. I spoke with the people from the real estate agency but it wasn't much help. Some of them were genuinely grief-stricken. Others are too scared to talk to an FBI agent out of fear of what it might do for sales. They did give me to key to the place, though."

DeMarco fished the key from her pocket as they climbed the porch steps. She unlocked the front door and they stepped inside. Kate found that the house had been totally moved out, not a speck of furniture in the place. There was also the smell of fresh paint and some sort of polish on the floor.

"And she was the second?" Kate asked as she closed the door behind them.

"Yes. The first was also a real estate agent, in a house just like this one. The first victim, though, was killed in a newer home. About two years old, I think. This house we're standing in right now is about fifteen years old."

"Anything of note regarding the personal lives of the victims?"

"Nothing yet. I've gone through background checks and had the help of the local PD in looking for arrest records. There's nothing…just a few speeding tickets and a single DWI charge. The families are no help either. We're being told they were both great women, wouldn't hurt a fly. That sort of thing."

Kate took a look around. There were blood splatters on the floor, just inside the entryway. A tall flight of stairs started just off of the foyer. There were smudges of dried blood on the hardwood stairs and even a dried stream of it running down the light teal paint on the wall that ran between the stairs and the ceiling. The stairs were the sort that were completely visible all the way to the second floor, a single thick railing breaking the space between the stairs and the open air.

Kate studied the pattern and trail of the blood and could not make immediate sense of it.

"Seems weird, right?" DeMarco said. "From what I've gathered, Tamara Bateman was attacked either on the stairs or at the very bottom. After that, she was dragged back to almost the very top of the stairs. She was then apparently thrown over the railing, with a noose attached to her neck. If you go up the stairs and have a look along the third step from the top, you can actually see pooled blood and what are very obviously rope fibers."

"She was hung?"

"Yes. And so was the first victim. Only, she was hung from a rafter that ran horizontally along the living room ceiling."

"Were the victims from the same real estate agency?" Kate asked.

"Nope. Different agencies. But both houses had been recently put on the market. That and the fact that both victims are female agents are the only links. I say *only*... but it seems like those links would be more than enough. But—as if evidenced by you being called out here—it's most definitely not."

"You been in here before now?" Kate asked.

"Yeah, yesterday afternoon. The body had been here for about twelve hours before anyone knew what had happened. Bateman's boyfriend called the police to voice his concern. A call was made to the agency, they found out the properties she was dealing in, and *voilà*... they found her hanging from the railing. I got here about eight hours after the body had been removed. You are more than welcome to look the place over. I promise you I won't be offended. I'll get you a copy of the coroner's report, too, but it says pretty much the same thing I just told you. When a woman is hit in the head and then hung, there's usually not much to add."

"Any sexual abuse from the killer?"

"Nothing showed up in the report. Seriously... the damned thing was no help at all."

Kate gave her a grin, though it was indeed an awkward situation. She felt like she was stepping on DeMarco's toes, poking her head in where it might not be wanted. Plus, it was the first case they worked together where DeMarco had been there first—where she more or less had the authority.

She headed up the stairs cautiously, keeping her eyes down to make sure not to step in any blood even if it was dry. She found the stair where the killer had apparently tossed the body over. There was a very slight abrasion on the finely polished railing. There were decorative spindles positioned every six inches or so, connecting the rail to the stairs. The spindle along this particular stair had a few strands of what looked like hair-thin burlap sticking to it. Or, as DeMarco had indicated, rope fabric. It was also resting on the edge of the stair, almost like dust.

Kate peered over the railing, to the floor. About a twelve-foot drop. This meant the noose had likely been very short. And if it had been short, there was a chance the killer had intentionally made it short—as if he had preplanned it, knowing where he would hang Tamara Bateman and how much rope he'd need.

"Got measurements on the noose?" Kate asked.

"The rope itself was eight feet long," DeMarco said. "Appeared to have been purchased at that length, as there was no clear sign of it having been cut."

Kate was impressed. The rope length was likely unimportant, but still a detail that would be necessary for an accurate and complete report. As she had expected, DeMarco had not missed a beat.

Kate continued up the stairs to the second floor. DeMarco trailed behind, being respectful and giving her ample space. There were five doorways along the upstairs hall: two on either side, and one at the end of the hallway. The hallway itself was not carpeted but the opened doors to all five rooms showed that the rooms (except the small bathroom at the end of the hall) were. Kate stepped into the first one. The house had apparently been cleaned and cared for quite well when the previous owners had moved out. There was not a single scratch on the walls and only the faintest indentations in the carpet to show that furniture had ever been there at all.

This bedroom was likely one of the guest rooms, as it was quite small. The only area to check other than the empty room itself was the closet. It was a small closet—no larger than a coat closet, really—and yielded nothing other than more very clean carpet. The next room was the same, as was the much larger master bedroom. The master bedroom also offered a large bathroom to look over, but it was just as sparkling clean as the rest of the house.

The third room they came to was more of the same, only the closet was much larger; it was a thin walk-in closet complete with clothes racks and a shelf for shoes. It was equally as empty as the other rooms, but there was another door sitting in the far wall. It was thinner than the others, located all the way in the corner of the spacious closet.

"Storage space?" Kate asked, walking toward the door.

"Yeah, I think so. It's a mostly unfinished attic space from the looks of it. I checked it yesterday."

Kate opened the door and was met with a blast of humid air. The space was indeed unfinished. There were exposed beams and insulation, broken only by the large air conditioning unit that had been installed in the space. The previous owners had laid down a few sheets of plywood to walk safely across the area, but that was about it. Near the back, the shape of the slanted roof narrowed the space. The builders had supported this with several boards, making sort of a faux wall. It was the only break in the perfectly square area.

Kate stepped out onto the plywood. As she walked across it, she thought it was a shame the space had gone to waste. If finished, it could have made a great office or playroom for a family with kids. Just as she started to envision where to install a set of stairs to cut away through the floor back to the main level, she came to the lazy unfinished wall near the back where the roof slanted down. She peered behind the would-be wall and cocked her head, puzzled.

"Did you look back here yesterday?" she asked.

DeMarco came walking across the plywood floor, curious and concerned. She looked, saw the same thing Kate was seeing, and uttered: "What the hell?"

There was a quilt lying on the plywood floor. An empty Dasani water bottle sat beside it, empty.

"Kate, I won't even lie to you. I didn't even think to look back there."

"No reason to," Kate said. "Not for anyone tasked with trying to figure this out all on their own. Chalk this one up to my overly analytical mind."

"Still. I should have looked."

"Could be a squatter," Kate pointed out, not wanting to give DeMarco time to be too hard on herself. "They tend to come and go, especially in properties that have been sitting stagnant for a while."

"Doubtful. The police were here all day yesterday, well into the night."

"Could be a squatter that kept eyes on the place, waiting for the police to leave. And if that's the case, the squatter could be the killer. Certainly would be one hell of a coincidence if this is here right now if it wasn't yesterday, considering someone was killed here less than two days ago."

"Someone would have to have been watching this house very closely, that's for sure."

Kate and DeMarco looked down to the meager sleeping area, their minds already kicking into gear. Kate couldn't help but think that if this quilt and bottle did indeed belong to the killer, she'd be heading back to Richmond before the day was over.

CHAPTER THREE

Small-town charm had never affected Kate, and Estes was no different. Sure, it was quaint and might be a nice place to spend a few weeks during the summer, but she could not imagine living in a place like this. She almost felt bad for the little town—its livelihood built around this beautiful but lesser-known lake, likely overshadowed by the beaches less than an hour and a half away. It was like the town had an identity crisis and wasn't even aware of it.

While DeMarco spoke to the local sheriff on the phone, Kate watched the town roll by, listening to one side of the conversation.

"We need at least one unit over at the house on Hammermill Street," DeMarco was saying. "If the killer was brave enough to sleep there and leave his quilt, there's a very good chance he might show back up. And even if it's not the killer, they might have seen or heard something."

Kate took the moment to appreciate the cadence with which DeMarco approached her job. Kate had given DeMarco bits of responsibility here and there during their time together as partners, but she had never gotten to see her in a leadership position. It seemed natural to her, the sudden lead in a case not shaking her a bit. She was working the case as if she'd led hundreds of them prior to this.

Kate listened in to the rest of the conversation as DeMarco made more suggestions and asked smart questions. After a while, DeMarco gave a curt little nod and a quick "Thank you" before hanging up.

"What's the police force like around here?" Kate asked.

"Pleasant enough. The sheriff is a fifty-something woman who loves the town and has a very motherly demeanor. The few officers under her that I've met seem to like her quite a bit."

"Have any of the other real estate agents spoken to the police?"

"Yeah, a few. The guy you and I are headed to see was the only one Sheriff Armstrong had any doubts about. She didn't let him know that, though. She wanted me to check in on him today."

"She say why she doubted his story?"

"She said when they got the call yesterday morning about Bateman going missing, some of the other agents said he seemed a little too eager to go check. I ran his record, too. He has a domestic abuse charge from a few years back somewhere in upstate New York."

"It would stand to reason that someone with working knowledge of current houses for sale would fit the bill for our killer," Kate said. "Someone who knows where agents will be, and when they'd be alone."

They drove several blocks down Estes's main stretch before DeMarco took a left and headed down a small row of gift shops, eateries, and so on. Right at the end of the block was a place called Lakeside Realty. They parked in a parking lot bordered with crossties and sand. Kate had to admit, the way the town was set up *did* make her yearn for the lake. She'd much rather have the beach, but she supposed that was a feeling most people in Estes felt from time to time.

They stepped inside the building and found a big lobby with an open-floor plan sitting beyond it separated by a bar-type counter that crossed the entire floor, broken by a cute little half-sized swinging door in the center. A woman sitting at a desk in the lobby greeted them kindly, doing her best to pretend she had not been gnawing on the donut that sat beside her before they had come in.

"Good morning, ladies," the woman said. "Can I help you?"

"We need to speak with Brett Towers, please," DeMarco said.

"Go on to the back then," the woman said. "He's the only one here this early."

They did as instructed, Kate making sure to stay behind DeMarco, not wanting to bully her way into the lead. Sure enough, as the woman up front had indicated, there was only one agent in the back. There were five desks taking up the large open area, and only one was occupied. A man—presumably Brett—was sitting behind his desk, sipping coffee and moving the mouse at his workstation around. He saw the agents approaching and quickly set his coffee mug down.

"Agent DeMarco, right?" Brett asked.

"Yes, that's right," she said. "I spoke with you on the phone briefly yesterday. This is my partner, Agent Wise."

Everyone shook hands as Brett Towers invited them to sit down across from his desk. "So please, let me know what I can do to help. Tamara and I were very close; we'd been with this agency for six years, right from the moment it started. It was just the two of us for a few months."

"So you were the first active agents working for Lakeside Realty?" DeMarco asked.

"That's right. Now, honestly, Tamara did try her hand at a competitor of ours, but that didn't last very long."

"Any idea why she jumped ship?" Kate asked.

"It was Crest Realty. They offered her more money but after a few months she came back. Said the atmosphere over there was too tense. She said it was more about the money than trying to find a right match for the clients."

"Did she have anything bad to say about anyone in particular?"

"No. And even if she did feel that way, she wouldn't have said anything. Tamara was an incredibly kind woman."

"Mr. Towers," Kate said, "did it come as a surprise to you to find that Tamara Bateman had been murdered? That is, can you think of any issues she might have had in the days or weeks leading up to her murder?"

"None at all. The police asked me the exact same question."

Kate could tell that Towers was not doing well. He was trying hard to hide some emotion, doing his very best to carry on. She hated to take such a tactic, but she figured if she could get him to drop the façade, it would be easier to get a read on him. She was also hoping that in a town the size of Estes, finding a killer would be a little easier if she was able to have people answer questions based on emotion. She knew it was a slightly sloppy tactic, but it worked more often than not.

"So I take it you and Ms. Bateman were close?" Kate asked.

"Yes, we were."

She heard a tremor in his voice, indicating that he was trying very hard not to break down and cry.

"Why on earth are you here at work this morning, then?" DeMarco asked. "You discovered the body, correct?"

"I did," he said. And then the tears came. His face tightened as he tried to keep a cork in. "But we're a small company, coming out of a successful summer in a lakeside community. With her gone, there's a ton of things I need to get wrapped up or it's going to fall through the cracks."

"Mr. Towers," DeMarco said, "I'm no therapist, but you saw her body before anyone else. That can be traumatic. It's okay to take some time ..."

"I plan on it. I'm skipping out of here at ten or so and taking the rest of the day. That's why I'm here so early. I hate to put business first, but with her no longer being here, there are lots of loose ends that need tying up as soon as possible."

"Are you capable of answering a few hard questions?" DeMarco asked.

"Absolutely. The cops told me this was the second agent that had been killed in six days. If I can help find who's doing this, yes ... ask me anything."

"What can you tell us about the home she was selling?" Kate asked. "Was it a well-known property? Is there any sort of history to it?"

"None that I'm aware of. Just a standard house."

"Did you know the previous residents?" DeMarco asked.

"Not personally, no. That property was Tamara's and solely hers. But even she probably wouldn't have met them because it was sold to a guy who buys and sells houses for a living. I can't remember his name."

"How long has the house been on the market?" Kate asked.

"It went on the market as soon as the new owner finished fixing it up—so about two weeks, I'd think. It's a gorgeous house—which is a shame."

"A shame?" DeMarco asked. "Why's that?"

"Because we have to disclose all information. Even if someone in Estes happens to *not* have heard about the brutal murder that occurred there, we'd have to tell them. It makes the house a lot harder to sell. And we're currently in a market that sees a lot of these bigger houses just sit and collect dust for months."

"Mr. Towers, do you know if Tamara was seeing anyone romantically? She wasn't married, right?"

"Right. And I don't think she was dating anyone. She tended to be sort of private about that. But I'll just say that if she *was* seeing someone, I didn't know about it."

Kate felt terrible for the man. He was doing everything he could to stay in control of himself, even as tears continued to roll down his face. Besides, she doubted they would get much useful information out of him anyway. She thought they could maybe use Tamara's records and clientele list from the last year or so, but that was a request they could leave with the woman at the front desk on their way out. As for Brett Towers, he'd already been through enough.

But Kate did not want to say anything. She wanted DeMarco to bring the discussion to its end, as this was her case and she had already spoken with him.

Apparently, she was on the same level as Kate. DeMarco got to her feet, and Kate followed suit.

"Thank you for your time, Mr. Towers," DeMarco said. "We may need to speak with you again, but for now, I think that's all."

He nodded, and Kate could see the relief on his face. When they left, she did leave a request with the woman at the front, asking if she could email them all records pertaining to showings, sales, and the complete list of clients Tamara Bateman had seen over the course of the last year.

When they stepped back outside, Kate found herself instantly headed for the driver's side. She corrected herself at the last minute and veered to the right, to the passenger's side.

DeMarco chuckled as she opened the driver's side door. "It's okay, Wise. You can drive and you can ask questions when we speak to people. I promise you ... you won't be stepping on my toes. We're partners, and this is no longer the Kristen DeMarco show. And like I said before, I'm glad to have you."

"That's good to hear," Kate said as she got into the car.

It was the truth; out of all of the current people in her life, DeMarco seemed the easiest to please. And as such, it made her enjoy the work that much more. She'd felt similar feelings about partners in the past and it had strained her marriage and her relationship with Melissa. She always kept that in the back of her head, making sure she didn't step across that line again. She knew she had already come close a few times since returning to duty, but she felt she was doing a better job of managing it now.

"Want to go check the crime scene of the first victim?" DeMarco asked.

"It's like you're in my head."

DeMarco gave a playful shudder. "Sometimes I wonder if that would be a wonderful place to be or a scary one."

"Depends on the day."

Kate had meant it as a joke but was a little alarmed that there was also a huge grain of truth to it. The past six weeks, with no work and only the pleasures of a plain life to distract her, had been rife with good days and bad—days when she was happy to be free of work and days when she missed it fiercely.

And now that she was working again, it felt *too* comfortable ... and she wasn't sure if that was a good thing or not.

CHAPTER FOUR

The house the first agent had been killed in was a bit larger than the one on Hammermill Street. It was located on a private lot just six miles away from the house Tamara Bateman had been killed in. The closest neighbor was about three hundred yards away, the homes separated by a thin copse of trees and wild weeds that looked like the beachgrass that often grew on sand dunes. This house also resembled a beach house, though also with certain elements of a farmhouse style.

As Kate and DeMarco climbed the stairs to the massive wrap-around porch, DeMarco handed Kate a folder she had taken from the back seat of the car. "You're going to want to see the photos to really get the full effect of this one. But...wait a second. Trust me."

DeMarco unlocked the front door (she'd apparently been given the key to this house as well) and led Kate inside. The front door opened onto a very large foyer—so large that a small loveseat sat against the right wall and an ornate rug the size of Kate's bedroom filled most of the floor. The rug was white and teal, allowing the dark red bloodstains to show up drastically.

Kate looked up and saw a huge open ceiling. In front of them, she could see the hallway to the second floor, blocked off by a beautiful interplay of a rail and decorative iron slats. A stairway led up to the second floor from the end of the foyer on the right. As she looked up those stairs, Kate noticed the beautiful chandelier hanging over the foyer. It looked to be made of some sort of steel, decorated in intricate twists to look almost like knots—like driftwood, almost. It was the perfect blend of beach house and farmhouse.

Along the base where it was installed into the ceiling, it looked to be slightly loose and askew.

"The chandelier," DeMarco said. "Pretty, isn't it?"

"It's gorgeous."

"Okay, now look inside the folder."

Kate did, skipping past the notes and police reports to get to the crime scene photos in the back. The first one showed the chandelier, only it looked much less beautiful. In fact, it looked like something out of a horror movie.

There was a body hanging from it. A rope was tied to the neck of the woman, but it looked like what was holding her up was the fact that her arms were caught on several of the chandelier's branches. In the picture, Kate could not see the end of the rope that was tied elsewhere. It looked to be going behind the chandelier, perhaps wrapped around the links that connected it to the ceiling.

The woman's face was a mess of blood and in the awkward pose as she hung from the chandelier, it appeared she was looking down directly toward the rug she was bleeding on. She was a small woman, her light weight not nearly enough to pull the huge chandelier from the ceiling.

"Jesus," Kate gasped. "How would someone even get her up there?"

"Well, the agent you're looking at is Bea Faraday. She's twenty-eight years old and weighs about one twenty. The cops seem to believe the killer hauled her up the stairs to the second floor and tossed her over the rail, attempting to hang her in the same way he eventually hung Tamara, but the chandelier got in the way."

"You buy it?" Kate asked.

"I do. There's blood on that upstairs rail to support it. I think that might be where he tied the rope at first, but then when he realized she was hanging from the fucking chandelier, he cut the rope and let the sight speak for itself. Looks like he attacked with her some blunt weapon first, then took the time to take her up the stairs and toss her over."

They walked to the top of the stairs and Kate found the spot where Faraday had apparently been tossed over. The chandelier was only about six feet away from the rail, the lights hanging just slightly below. She had no problem imagining a strong man being able to launch a small woman that far.

"How was she found?" Kate asked.

"The agency sent a cleaning woman to do a quick sweep of the place two hours before a scheduled showing. The cleaning lady found her and called the police."

"Have you spoken to her?"

"No. Sheriff Armstrong has, though."

Kate nodded, looking down onto the first floor and the blood-stained rug. She was thinking about the quilt and water bottle they had found at the house on Hammermill Street, wondering if there were nooks and crannies within this home that might allow a squatter to hide away rather easily.

"How old is this house?" Kate asked.

"Not sure. But it's been on the market for the better part of a month. Records show that it had been shown eighteen times, with six potential buyers. Only one of the potential buyers was a local."

Kate and DeMarco walked through the house, their footfalls echoing in the empty rooms. Kate thought it was an eerie feeling, actually—the feel of a house that held the memories and lives of people she would never meet. She'd always been vaguely interested in ghosts and found it entirely possible that every house had the potential to be haunted by the memories and motions of the families who had lived within it.

They checked the large space that Kate assumed served as the living room area, and then the kitchen. Being that there were no belongings of any kind in the place, it was quite easy to determine that nothing had been taken. They then made their way upstairs. Kate was looking for some sort of easy access to an attic or even little eaves spaces. But there was nothing of the sort. The house did not have an attic, which, to Kate, meant it likely had a basement of some kind. No one built houses in communities like these anymore without at least some form of extra storage space.

They headed back downstairs and headed for the first door along the main hallway. It led down to a finished basement that was just as vacant and desolate as the rest of the home. To the back, there was a set of double doors that presumably led outside. Kate went to them, opened the doors, and indeed found herself looking out onto a gorgeously green backyard. She stepped out, DeMarco following behind her, onto a patio that was the shape of a half oval. To the right was slightly raised brick wall that contained a flower bed. To the left was a small unstructured space beneath a set of wooden stairs that led up to the back porch. The space she assumed was to install something like a small storage shed for a lawnmower, mulch bags, and things of that nature.

Going on a hunch, she walked to the unfinished space. The dirt underneath it was hard packed and dry, levelled out from the landscaping prior to the house being built. She knelt down and checked the ground over, not sure what she was looking for. She nearly came away with nothing, but just before she pulled back, she caught sight of something in the back far corner immediately to her left, almost completely out of her sight.

Grunting a bit from the amount of stretching she had to do to see back into it, she saw what looked to be several old shop rags. They were bundled into something that resembled a pile, one on top of the other. A few feet down from the cloths, she saw what looked like scuff marks in the dirt.

"Anything?" DeMarco asked.

"Maybe. Why don't you have a look and tell me what you see … just to make sure I'm not jumping to conclusions."

The women switched places and Kate watched as DeMarco hunched her much younger back over so that her body was almost in an L-shape. She scurried into the unfinished space and looked around for a moment before saying anything.

"Shop rags," she called out from within the space. "Seems like a weird thing to leave behind in this space, right? And … yeah, and a few scuffs and indentations in the ground here. It's dry but I'm pretty sure some amount of weight was placed here sometime recently."

DeMarco came back out, stretching her back. "The cloths," she said. "You think someone used them as a pillow or something?"

"I do."

"Another squatter? Seems like a stretch. But yes, those slight marks on the ground could have been the bending of a knee or the placement of a foot, I guess." She eyed them once more and added: "And recently, too."

"It does seem like a desperate stretch to make," Kate agreed. "Especially given that the heap of old cloths could easily be nothing more than lazy clean-up by the construction crew."

"I'd like to speak to the cleaning lady," DeMarco said.

"That's a good idea—the next logical step, I think."

"I'll call the real estate company to see if I can get an address. If not, I'm sure Sheriff Armstrong would help us out."

DeMarco turned her back to do just that, walking to the edge of the concrete patio and looking out over the backyard. As she spoke, Kate looked back into the unfinished space beneath the stairs and the side of the house. She tried bending like DeMarco but simply did not have that kind of flexibility anymore. She got to her knees and waddled into the space, looking for anything else they might have missed. She found nothing new, but the more she looked at the pile of rags and the slight disturbances to the ground, the more certain she became that someone had been resting there within the past few days. She made a mental note to bag up the rags to check for hair fibers.

As she was coming back out of the little space under the stairs, DeMarco was pocketing her phone.

"Get an address?" Kate asked.

"Even better. Turns out she's been called to the police station. Armstrong called her in for additional questioning. I just spoke to Armstrong and she said she's fine if we come by to take part."

"Sounds good to me," Kate said, trying to hide the grimace of pain that crept across her face as she once again righted herself after coming out of the small space.

As she followed behind DeMarco while they cut around the house through the yard, she couldn't help but smile. DeMarco had really taken control of the case and was managing to continue making it her own even after Kate had been called in. Smiling, Kate found that she was too proud of DeMarco to feel the least bit slighted.

When they arrived at the station, just a quarter of a mile away from the still waters of Fallows Lake, Sheriff Armstrong was in the front lobby, waiting to greet them. She looked rather relieved to see them, not quite smiling at them but certainly pleased. She appeared to be in her early fifties and had a bit of heft to her, but was far from being considered overweight. She had a plain face that was likely pretty when her hair was up and some makeup was applied. What Kate liked the most about her, though, was that she had a serious glint in her eyes... the look of a woman who took her job and her duties very seriously.

"I was very happy to hear you were headed over," Armstrong said. "I have Ms. Seibert in the back. She's starting to get very defensive. I have no reason to believe she had anything to do with the murders, but she *thinks* we see her as a suspect just because we called her back in."

"I wonder if there's a history of crime in her family," Kate said. She then grinned when Armstrong looked at her, puzzled. "Sorry," Kate said. "Agent Kate Wise. Pleased to meet you."

"Same here," Armstrong said. "As for your question, I honestly don't know."

"It happens a lot," Kate explained. "If she's seen a family member or two in problems with the authorities, the chances are very good she's going to be defensive no matter how nicely she's treated."

"Well, I've given her five minutes to cool down. I told her someone else might step in to ask some questions and she wasn't too keen on that."

"You mind if we take over?" DeMarco asked.

"Not at all. Down the hallway, third room on the left."

Kate and DeMarco headed in that direction. Kate noticed that she had somehow stepped in front but did not want to go out of her way to correct it. When they reached the door Armstrong had indicated, Kate gave a brief knock, waited two seconds, and then opened the door.

There was only a table and a few chairs occupying the room. The woman sitting at the table looked to be in her late fifties, maybe early sixties. She was a Caucasian woman with stringy hair that poked up in little frazzles here and there. She eyed Kate and DeMarco suspiciously, her eyes darting back and forth between them.

"You're Mary Siebert?" DeMarco asked.

Mary only nodded. Kate saw right away that Armstrong had been right; the woman looked like she was expecting the absolute worst.

"We're Agents DeMarco and Wise, with the FBI. We were hoping to ask you some questions about your discovery of the body of Bea Faraday."

Again, Mary said nothing. She sat a little more rigidly in her chair but other than that, she remained mostly unchanged.

"Ms. Seibert," DeMarco went on, "Sheriff Armstrong tells us that you feel like you're a suspect. We're here to tell you that as of right now, that's just not the case. We have such an interest in you because you were the first one on the scene. And also because with your profession, we are hoping you might have seen or heard something lately that could help us on the case. Nothing more. We'd like to speak to you so we can work towards trying to determine how long the body had been there before you arrived, maybe if you saw anything else odd, things like that."

Mary started to loosen up a bit. Kate marveled at how well DeMarco was doing. She had not only worked to ease Mary's fears, but she had also subtly made the woman feel like what she had to contribute was very important—which it was.

"No, there was just the body," Mary said. "And all that blood."

"Did you know Ms. Faraday at all?" Kate asked.

"No. Although later, when I saw pictures of her, I recognized her face. I'd seen her around the town, you know? It's a beautiful town, but not very big."

"And you were alone, right?" DeMarco asked.

"Yes, it was just me."

"How many others work for the cleaning company?"

"There are five of us. But because this house had been stripped of most of the furniture and hadn't seen much foot traffic in a while, I was the only one that went. It was to be a simple mop and dust job. The windows hadn't even gotten any smears or grime on them yet."

DeMarco flipped through the file folder on the table. "And you arrived at two fifteen in the afternoon, correct?"

"Yes. I had one other house to visit that day. But I obviously didn't make it."

"This might sound like a disturbing question," Kate said, "but do you happen to recall if the blood was still wet?"

"Oh, sure. It was still wet. There was still blood dripping from the body. As weird as it seems ... that's the thing that keeps me from sleeping at night. It's not the poor woman's face or even the gross scene itself; it's the sound that fresh blood made when it splattered on the floor—that dripping sound."

"So, Ms. Siebert ... who makes the calls requesting you come out to clean the house?"

"The real estate agency."

"And which agency was this house with?" DeMarco asked.

"Davis and Hopper Realty."

"Have they been a client of yours for very long?" Kate asked.

"Maybe two years. They pay well and the agents working over there are some of the nicest people you'll ever meet."

There was silence in the room for a moment as Kate and DeMarco both worked out their own trains of thought in their head. Meanwhile, Mary Seibert seemed quite relaxed—a far cry from the woman Sheriff Armstrong had described to them less than ten minutes ago. It was Kate who eventually broke the silence. She had decided there was no way Mary Seibert had killed Bea Faraday, hauled her up the stairs, and then tossed her limp body at least six feet across the open air from the second-floor rail. There was just no way.

"Ms. Seibert, had you ever been in the house before?"

"No, this was the first time."

"And while you were there," DeMarco said, "did you happen to see anything else? Maybe some kind of sign someone else might have been there?"

"Like I said... all I saw was the body. Well, I saw the blood on the floor first, right when I walked into the house, and then I saw her body up there on the chandelier. I sort of went blank for a few seconds, I think. I remember finding it very hard to breathe and then, when I could breathe, I screamed. I ran outside and called the police. They asked me to wait in my car, so that's what I did."

DeMarco glanced over at Kate. Kate gave her a nod at the same time she flashed Mary Seibert a smile. DeMarco was the first to head for the door, giving Mary her own smile as she did so.

"How long have you been cleaning homes in the area?" Kate asked.

"About eight or nine years."

"In all of that time, have you ever happened upon anything even remotely like this before?"

"Oh, every now and then we'll come to a home that has very clearly been used. Usually it's just teenagers looking for a place to party. Every now and then we'll find evidence of people sleeping on the floors. I had a friend one time that walked into a house one morning and found a homeless man sleeping in the back closet of a bedroom."

"That was here in Estes?" DeMarco asked.

"No, somewhere out near New Castle."

Kate and DeMarco shared a glance, one that they had both come to know and understand from the other during their time together. It was a look that said: *"This interview is over."*

"Thank you so much for your time, Ms. Seibert. Unless Sheriff Armstrong needs anything from you, I'd say you're free to go. We appreciate your cooperation."

Mary stood up, obviously ready to make her way out. "I hear there's been another one. Is that right?"

"We can't give explicit details just yet," DeMarco said. She started through the door but then paused, turned back, and added: "But I'd suggest staying away from any houses that are currently for sale until you hear otherwise."

"We may also be passing along the same warning to all real estate employees in the area," Kate said.

Mary nodded, looking to the table as if she wasn't sure what to think. Kate had seen the expression many times before. It was the look of a woman who loved the little town she called home, but was starting to understand that it was no longer as safe as she had once thought.

CHAPTER FIVE

Kate discovered very quickly that she liked Sheriff Armstrong quite a lot. She was a well-grounded woman who did not take her job too seriously. When she sat down with Kate and DeMarco at a small conference room in the back of the building fifteen minutes after Mary Seibert had been excused, she did so with the gait of a stressed teenage kid. The woman was likely somewhere between fifty and fifty-five years of age, but the uncertain look on her face made her look much younger. She was pretty in a plain way, taking in both agents with a pair of radiant green eyes.

"You know," she said, holding a cup of coffee with both hands as she reclined back in her chair, "I really wish you two could have visited the area for other reasons. Have either of you ever been to Estes or anywhere else around the area?"

Kate and DeMarco both answered in the negative. Kate was sipping from her own cup of coffee that Armstrong had offered, running the few facts of the case over in her mind. She studied the room closely as she did so, as she assumed this would likely serve as their primary hub of operations until this case was closed.

There was a large map of the area on the far wall, directly beside a dry-erase board. The board looked as if it wasn't used very often, the most incriminating piece of evidence coming from a scrawled date that had only been partially erased in the right upper corner from almost an entire year ago.

"Well, I'm here to serve," Armstrong said. "Other than these two murders, we've been pretty quiet around here lately. It's sort of a cushy job. Even when the summer brings in the tourists, it remains a mostly quiet town. A few speeding tickets and bar brawls on Saturday nights, but that's about it. So obviously, everything this week has been…"

She trailed off here, as if not even wanting to attempt to find the appropriate word to finish the statement.

DeMarco looked to Kate, hitching her thumb back toward Armstrong. "She and a few officers already have just about everything we could need here—files, reports, sales listings, things like that. I've worked with her a bit but not much—just an hour or so yesterday."

"Do you happen to have a current list of all of the houses for sale in the area?" she asked.

"I do," Armstrong said. "It came through this morning after I got on the line and demanded every real estate company in the area provide their listings ASAP. The list is in my office, but I can email it to you as well."

"How long is it?"

"In the town of Estes, there are currently sixteen homes for sale and five for rent. If you venture out of Estes and go all the way out to the lake, the number gets much larger. Forty-one for sale, nineteen for rent."

Kate got to her feet and went to the map on the wall. She glanced it over for a few seconds and found Estes near the top right corner of the map. "Where on here is Hammermill Street?"

"Oh God, you'll go blind using that." She leaned in her chair, closer to the door, and yelled: "Hey, Jimmy! Get me the topographical map of Estes!"

An obedient *"On it!"* boomed out from elsewhere in the office. The whole exchange was funny and, in a strange way, a bit refreshing for Kate. She'd always had a warm feeling toward small-town police forces, and Estes was no exception.

"I've thought of that, too," Armstrong said. "The neighborhoods are pretty similar. The houses, too, I guess—only one was brand new and the other not so much. Different agencies, which makes me think the agencies won't be a link."

"Stairs were used in both murders," DeMarco pointed out. "It makes me think the killer had to know where the stairs would be before entering the homes in order to pull it off."

"We also think there might have been a squatter in both properties," Kate said. "We're not one hundred percent certain yet, but there's enough there to seriously pursue it."

"What sort of evidence?" Armstrong asked.

As DeMarco started telling her, a young officer Kate assumed to be Jimmy entered the office with a large map in his hands. He was already unfolding it for them, placing it on the table. He did so a bit clumsily, covering the files that were already there.

"Thank you, Jimmy," Armstrong said in a way that indicated she wanted him out of there as soon as possible.

Jimmy nodded, looked at both Kate and DeMarco (his eyes lingering a bit longer on DeMarco), and then took his exit.

"I repeat," Armstrong said, noting the way Kate had looked at Jimmy, "it's a quiet little town. We don't necessarily need the roughest and toughest."

The three women snickered as they got to their feet and situated themselves around the map of Estes. The streets were laid out perfectly, the crisscrossing oddly peaceful in Kate's mind.

"Here's Hammermill," Armstrong said, pointing with a marker. She placed an X on the street and said, "This is the site of the most recent murder. And here," she said, scanning the map and then placing another X, "is the site of the first murder. Leander Drive, about six miles away."

Kate looked at the two X's, knowing it was too soon to really take a pattern away from the location. Of course, she hoped they could find their killer before any sort of pattern could start to emerge.

"I'd like to—" Kate started, but was cut off by her phone. She checked it, saw that it was Allen, and nearly ignored it. But given the way her job had affected their relationship, that was the last thing she needed to do. She had to show him that he was a priority in her life...even when he called out of the blue and interrupted important meetings.

A bit reluctantly, she kept the phone out and looked to DeMarco and Armstrong. "Excuse me a moment, would you?"

She stepped out into the hallway and took a few steps away from the conference room door before answering. When she finally did, she tried her best not to sound as irritated as she felt. "Hey there."

"Hey yourself," Allen said. "I thought I'd let you know I'm all checked in. I met with one of the guys from the company I'm out here to see and he already has the next three days planned out. But already... based on just one conversation, he says he has a good feeling about this."

"That's great." But really, even she could hear the distance in her voice. And if she could hear it, she knew *he* could hear it.

"Sorry... you're busy, aren't you?"

"Yeah. Two murders, no leads."

His sigh coming from the other end of the line might as well have been him uttering a curse at her. "Sorry I bothered you."

"That's a nasty tone," Kate said.

"I didn't mean for it to be."

"How's the meeting going?" she asked, wanting to seem supportive and not sound like she had no time to be on the phone.

"It's okay. I'm just nervous. Things have gone well so far but... you know what? Let's just wait. You're busy and ..."

"I am. But that's okay."

"It's just that if this meeting goes well, I could retire with a very nice chunk of change through a sizable bonus. You know that, right?"

"I do. And I want only the best for you and hope you get it. But I have things going on here, too."

"Yeah, I'm used to that and... you know what? It's not worth arguing about. Let's just touch base when we're both back home. Sound good? You live your life, I'll live mine, and we'll keep them just as far apart as we possibly can."

"Allen, you—"

"Gotta go," he said.

And just like that, the call was over. Kate stared at the phone for a moment, trying to remember if there had ever been a moment in their relationship where Allen had actually hung up on her. The anger that flared up in her was only momentary, dwarfed by the guilt of choosing work over him yet again.

She pocketed her cell phone and headed back into the conference room. Armstrong and DeMarco were still standing over the map, Armstrong running her finger along a certain route.

"Sorry about that," Kate said.

"No worries," Armstrong said. "What were you saying before you stepped out?"

Kate had to throw her mind into reverse just to grasp the train of thought she had been on. When she found it, the emotions regarding Allen slid away quickly, throttled by the excitement of figuring out the puzzle of this case.

"I was going to say that I'd like to get a list of available properties that are located between the two houses where the murders occurred. If this squatter theory holds any weight, I'd say the chances are good that he or she is scanning that particular area."

Armstrong nodded, apparently liking the idea. "That's a great start... but why that area? Why would the killer—or even just a squatter—be interested in that area?"

"No clue," Kate said. "So I guess that's one of the things we need to figure out."

CHAPTER SIX

It took about twenty minutes for the three of them to pick the properties from the much longer list the three local agencies had provided the police department with. Another ten minutes, and Armstrong had marked each location on the map. In the area sitting between the two homes, there were eleven homes for sale and two for rent. As Kate and DeMarco prepared to head out and start investigating each property, Armstrong compiled a small force in the station. Armstrong would lead this group in finding out how old each property was, and how long they had been on the market. She also sent two other officers out to help shorten the search of the properties for Kate and DeMarco.

The clock had inched by noon as Kate and DeMarco arrived at the first house on the list. It was located a mile and a half away from the brand new build that Bea Faraday had been killed in. This house was not a new build and was described in the real estate listing as having been built in 1995. Located in an older subdivision, it was not nearly as expensive as the two murder scenes. Like the others, though, it was decorated for the lakeside or beach, with lots of driftwood, sand dollars, and teal-colored décor.

But that was all they found there. While there was a basement area that had been recently cleared out, there was no indication that a squatter—or anyone else, for that matter—had recently been there.

The second house on the list was just three blocks away from the first. It was a large property that was rented out over the summer and, until recently, had been lived in during the off-summer

41

months. Lakeside Realty currently represented the property, having placed it on the market four days ago. Based on the absolutely ridiculous price, Kate did not find it hard to believe that no one had showed any real interest in the place just yet. It wasn't even *on* the lake. She wasn't sure what the real estate strategies were when it came to the land developers in Estes, but it made no sense to Kate.

With five bedrooms, two office spaces, an enormous finished basement, and a crawlspace beneath, the property took far too long to look over. But they were thorough, checking every room and potential hidden space. But, as with the first home, there was nothing there.

As Kate and DeMarco got into the car, DeMarco's phone rang. After checking the display, she looked to Kate. "It's Armstrong."

As DeMarco answered the call, Kate listened in. The conversation was brief, and although she only heard DeMarco's end of the conversation, she was able to piece it all together.

"Well, you're going to have to tell them to wait...yes, I understand that. No, I don't think we need to suspend all real estate transactions for the time being...Thank you. Yes, we'll touch base by the end of the day."

DeMarco ended the call and reclined her head against the headrest of the passenger seat. "It's been exactly two hours since we asked for full access to the listed homes and two of the real estate companies are asking if they can schedule showings yet."

"Business and money trump human safety every time," Kate said. "It's sad, but true. Now...ready for the third house?"

"Sure," DeMarco said, pulling up the address. "By the way, two of Armstrong's guys have checked over three houses. Nothing worth noting at any of them. I'm really afraid this is going to turn out to be a waste of time."

"By ruling each listing out, it's not wasting time...it's knocking a to-do off of the list. And in a smaller community like this, we're going to have to do quite a bit of the heavy lifting."

She almost added, *Don't get so discouraged,* but decided against it. She didn't want to come off as some cheesy coach.

Instead, she guided the car out of the driveway and toward the next property on the list.

The third home they checked over was almost exactly between the two crime scene homes. The house stood on a stretch of land that seemed to run between two small subdivisions. It was on the side of the quaint stretch of road that led to several of the lake's loading areas and docks; the backyard was decorated in beach grass, giving it the appearance that it was not a lake that waited not too far away, but the ocean. The house itself was rather quaint, nothing special but very warm and cozy.

DeMarco unlocked the real estate agency's hide-a-key box on the front porch and unlocked the front door with the key that was sitting inside. The house was fully furnished—the first of its kind Kate had seen since arriving in Estes—and had been recently cleaned. She could smell the chemical scent of cleaning spray and a subtle undertone of bleach. She wondered if Mary Siebert or any of her co-workers had been the ones to clean it.

From the front door, they stepped directly into the living room. There was a built-in fireplace to the far right, and a huge sliding glass door that looked out to the backyard. To the left, there was a spacious kitchen and a hallway that branched off of it. They checked the immediate spaces and then, finding nothing, went into the hallway. Only a single bedroom sat along the small hallway and it was empty—the single room in the house that was not furnished. The carpet had obviously been cleaned recently, but the slight indentations of past furniture could be seen here and there.

They took the wide flight of stairs off of the hallway to the second floor. DeMarco was in the lead, and Kate followed a few stairs behind her. She was not paying very close attention, assuming this would play out just like the previous two properties. When searching countless homes, all of which were unoccupied, it was far too easy to fall into a formulaic sense of security.

But then DeMarco stopped, nearly at the top of the stairs, and shouted: "Hold it!"

At first, Kate thought the demand was being directed toward her. But the two words were immediately followed by the sound of fleeing footsteps, pounding along the second-floor hallway. DeMarco went running in pursuit, leaping up the last few stairs. Kate followed as fast as she could, coming to the top of the stairs just in time to see DeMarco take a hard left turn into the first bedroom in the upstairs hallway.

Unsure of what exactly DeMarco was going after, Kate drew her sidearm. Just as she reached the doorway, she heard a *thud*, the unmistakable sound of someone being punched. She heard DeMarco cry out just before she entered the room. When Kate stepped inside, she saw DeMarco on the floor, getting up. On the other side of the room, a man was ducking out of a window.

"Freeze," Kate said, pointing her Glock in the man's direction.

But the man had no intention of stopping. As his one remaining leg started to be pulled out of the window, Kate considered putting a round in his knee. But even she knew that was a bit over the top—for now. If she shot the man and it turned out he was nothing more than a squatter or someone who had broken into the home just for the hell of it, the aftermath could be very bad for her.

Instead, Kate dashed to the window and, without even thinking about it, followed after him. There were no curtains or blinds, so she could see the man perfectly as he neared the edge of the roof. He glanced around, then apparently saw something to the right. As he started darting in that direction, running cautiously along the slightly slanted roof that overhung the front porch, Kate recalled seeing a two-car garage attached to the house.

Kate stepped out onto the roof, having to holster her weapon to get out without stumbling over the window frame. As soon as she was out, her entire body froze for a moment. She saw the yard below her, the bright green grass and the street beyond. But once her eyes and brain decided that she really wasn't that high up at all (maybe fifteen feet), she chased after him. It wasn't until her feet were moving that she realized just what the hell she was doing. Fifteen feet or not…if she slipped and fell, she had a fairly significant drop waiting for her—a drop that, at her age, would at the very least break something.

But by the time this realization sank in, she was already halfway across the roof. And the man, standing at the edge and looking down to the separate, lower section of the garage roof, was the one who now appeared to be frozen.

"I'd think long and hard about that," Kate said.

It was as if her voice broke him out of his frozen state. For a moment, it looked like he might leap down onto the garage roof. But at the last moment, he changed his mind and dropped to his hands and knees. He moved fast, sliding his legs over the edge to dangle over the garage roof. But Kate was faster as she rushed forward.

She reached him before he was able to drop safely to the garage roof. She grabbed the one remaining arm that was clutching the roof and tried to pull him up. When she realized he was a bit too heavy for that, she locked his arm under her right arm and then, taking a deep breath and making sure not to look down, she jumped down into the garage roof.

It was less than a four-foot drop but she was still somehow convinced that it was at least twenty. When her feet hit the garage roof, the man's arm was still trapped between her right arm and her side. Her knees jarred a bit and there was a slight stinging pain in her right knee. But the adrenaline rushing through her controlled all of that.

By jumping, she had wrenched his arm painfully around, bringing him to his knees. Because the garage roof was much less angled than the porch roof—almost straight in the center, in fact—she was able to easily stand and push him down. He fought against her, but not much; it seemed as if he was much more scared of heights than Kate was.

"Want to tell me why you were running?" Kate asked.

"I didn't do anything wrong," the man said. He appeared to be in his late twenties or early thirties. He wore a black T-shirt and a pair of old tattered cargo shorts.

"Running away, punching my partner, and then jumping out onto a roof to escape would indicate otherwise," Kate said.

"Kate?"

Kate looked up and to the left, still holding the man's arm and pushing him lightly down onto the roof. DeMarco was hanging half out of the window, an amazed and puzzled look on her face.

"We're good," Kate said. "I'm going to let him decide...I can either toss him off the roof or he can come back inside with me." She pressed down on his arm a bit more. He tried to fight but, at the same time, also pushed back from the edge of the roof, which waited less than two feet from them. "Your choice," Kate said.

"Inside," he said, gritting his teeth from the pressure Kate was applying to his arm. "Just get me off of this roof!"

"Excellent choice," Kate said. She yanked him up by the same arm and twisted it up behind his back. "Now get moving."

When Kate and DeMarco brought the man to the station, Armstrong did not seem all that surprised. In fact, she looked at the man the same way someone might look at an irksome swarm of flies that was ruining a picnic.

Even before the suspect could be hauled into a room for questioning, Armstrong joined them in the hallway, hands on her hips and steel in her eyes.

"Where'd you find him?" Armstrong asked.

"A house on Edgecrest Street," DeMarco said. "Throws one hell of a right hook."

"You look like you know him," Kate said suspiciously.

"Oh yeah, I know him," she said. "Come this way, please."

Armstrong led them down the hallway and into a very small office space that apparently served as an interrogation room of sorts. Kate led the man by gently pushing him along. His hands were cuffed behind his back and he proceeded without any hesitation. It was almost as if he had been through all of this before.

When all four of them were in the room, Armstrong closed the door behind them. As Kate sat the man down in one of the room's three chairs (there was no desk or table), Armstrong leaned against the door.

"Ladies, this is Greg Seamster. Sort of a vagrant. He and I see a lot of one another... don't we, Greg?"

"Sheriff, I swear, I didn't do anything! I just needed somewhere to stay!"

Ignoring Greg, DeMarco looked to Armstrong for confirmation. "What sort of a record does he have?"

"It's a long one. Breaking and entering, loitering, petty theft, public intoxication."

"Homeless?" Kate asked.

"Yes."

"That's why I was in the house," Greg said. He was desperate sounding, almost like a young kid getting defensive. Kate thought there was a chance there might be some sort of mental disability at play.

"Greg, we've been over this," Armstrong said. "It wasn't your house."

"But no one was living there! I wasn't hurting anyone."

"That's true," Kate said. "But you did throw a punch at Agent DeMarco. She's a federal agent and you attacked her. That's rather serious, Mr. Seamster."

"Sheriff," DeMarco said, "I take it this isn't an isolated incident?"

"No. Unfortunately, we've caught Greg housing down in places he shouldn't on several occasions. Sometimes on people's porches, in a car one time, and yeah, a few times in a vacant rental property. But I have to tell you, Agents... he's never done anything that would lead me to believe he'd the one we're looking for."

"I'm really sorry," Greg said, looking to them, his eyes ping-ponging back and forth between the three women. "I usually sleep somewhere along the edge of the lake, but when the tourists aren't around it gets sort of scary."

Kate turned to face the wall, mainly to hide her disappointment. Yes, there was certainly some sort of mental condition at play here. It made her wonder why he was not somewhere to receive help rather than wandering the streets of Estes and the surrounding areas.

As she got her thoughts under control, she listened to DeMarco do her best to salvage the conversation. "Mr. Seamster, where else have you been sleeping lately?"

He was quiet, prompting Kate to turn around. He was looking at them as if he did not trust them. He looked almost pleadingly at Armstrong.

"It's okay, Greg," Armstrong said. "Look, you may be in some trouble for punching Agent DeMarco, but we won't press any charges for the sleeping situation—though you and I are going to need to have a conversation about that. Maybe even with your mother."

He nodded gravely and then looked at Kate and DeMarco. "The house you found me in today…I've been there for three nights. I usually leave during the day but I slept too late today…and usually they don't do any showings until later in the day."

"And what about before that house?" Kate asked.

"A few nights at my mom's house, one night on a bench out on the public loading area right by the lake over by Harker's View. There were a few nights the nice man over at the Lake Breeze Hotel let me have a room. But he stopped doing that."

Kate nodded and then looked to Armstrong. "Can we speak to you out in the hall?"

Armstrong nodded, looking as if she had been expecting this exact request. The three women filed out of the room and clustered together in the hallway.

"What's his story?" Kate asked.

"It's a pretty bad one. He technically lives with his mother, but it's a terribly strained relationship. I'm sure you can tell that he has some mental issues, but honestly, aside from the charges I told you about, he's not a bad guy. Every single one of the charges on his record is the result of his mental issues and neglect from his mother."

"From the way you're speaking to him, it sounds as if he's been busted for squatting before," Kate said.

"He has. I can look into his story. If Sam over at the Lake Breeze Hotel can verify when he was allowing Greg to keep a room, it could eliminate him."

"That would be appreciated," DeMarco said.

This spurred a thought in the back of Kate's mind. She let it linger there for a moment as she started to dissect it.

"Do you need me to hold Greg any further?" Armstrong asked.

"I don't think so," DeMarco said. She looked to Kate for confirmation, and Kate gave a shake of her head.

Armstrong looked appreciative, giving a quick little nod as she opened the door and walked back in to speak with Greg. Kate couldn't help but think she had taken a swing and missed—and that she might be in Estes a bit longer than she had hoped.

CHAPTER SEVEN

Most people enjoyed the sunsets and sunrises over the lake. He supposed he understood that; there was a simple beauty to the play of faded colors of light dancing on the water. And sometimes, especially in the mornings, it could look like something right out of a dream.

But he preferred the midday. Even now, as summer came to its end, there was still an oppressive heat. He had not lived at the lake for very long, but he knew there was some special way the heat seemed to enhance the smell of the water; it was fishy and sort of muddy but not in an unpleasant way. Even from where he was parked, about a mile away from the lake, he could smell it on the air. The sky was a perfect powder-blue, a meager little breeze pushing the scent through the open windows of his car.

The car was facing a large house that sat on the edge of a cul-de-sac. It had been placed on the market two days ago, but he had been watching the same real estate agent go inside for several days now. She was quite pretty, but in a mousy sort of way. She was also very conservative, dressing in a way that showed no cleavage and very little leg. She also wore her hair down, as if to cover up any portion of her neck that might be showing.

As he watched the house, he also spied the car currently pulling into the driveway. The house was enormous, and the two-car garage looked more like a four-car garage when the agent parked her little Nissan in front of it. The car sat there for about a minute before the driver's side door opened and the agent got out.

Her name was Dhayna Tsui, and she was a petite Asian woman. He knew nothing about her other than the way she looked and that she was an employee of Crest Realty. He also knew her schedule, as he had been following her for the last few days. She was preparing to show the house she was walking into, though not today. There was still no FOR SALE sign in the yard, just one of those little clear-sleeved signs that offered a printout of the house's details.

And really, that was all he needed to know.

He sat in his car and waited for her to go inside. He then thought briefly of his mother, wishing she was still with him. Of course, he had grown up and moved away from home years ago, but she had died five months ago and there were times where he could feel her absence like a cancer tearing through his body.

He watched the real estate agent closely, noticing that after unlocking the house and stepping inside, she took the little hide-a-key with her. That likely meant this was going to be a quick trip; he'd seen similar methods and shortcuts with the other two women he had followed and thought he knew the routines well.

Having the hide-a-key with her meant several things: first, she was not staying long; second, the door was not locked. If it was like the case with the woman he had accidentally gotten stuck in the stupid chandelier, the door might not even be all the way closed.

It was almost too easy.

He grabbed the piece of lumber he had taken from the first house, the one on Leander Drive. He'd been keeping it stowed beneath the passenger seat of his car ever since, blood stains and all. He reached under the seat again and took out the rope.

He had already tied it into a noose.

He hefted the piece of scarred lumber in his hand for a moment and then got out of the car. When he walked down the sidewalk—the yard to both sides recently cut and seeded—he knew the house was not a new build. It was about five or six years old according to the detail sheets contained within the plastic sleeve on the Realtor sign out front.

Aside from the things he was carrying in his hands, he might look like any random and uninteresting person heading inside to check out the house. And that's exactly how he wanted it to appear.

He walked up the porch in the same way, with a slight bounce in his step, and saw he had been correct... Dhayna had not closed the door all the way. She really did intend to be out of here quickly. She was probably just taking a few pictures of some of the rooms.

He made his way into the house. It opened up to a large foyer that presented a staircase almost right away. It was a gorgeous house, likely owned by someone with a considerable amount of money. And he was willing to bet that the owner was only selling it to make *more* money. Assholes like that only bought houses to improve upon them and then sell them again. They did not need a home or a shelter. As far as he was concerned, it was the very height of arrogance.

But he had no time to dwell on such things. He could instantly hear footsteps coming from the other side of the stairway, the sound of heels clicking on hardwood.

He went in that direction and saw her standing by the counter in the kitchen. Her back was to him, which made his job much easier.

He raised the piece of lumber as if it were a baseball bat and swung.

In the final moment, just before the wood connected with her head, he thought she had heard him moving. There had been the slightest little tilt of her head, but that had been it.

The lumber connected, rocking her head hard to the right and filling the kitchen with a sound very similar to the cracking of a baseball into center field.

Dhayna hit the counter and rebounded to the floor. She was whimpering, making odd sounds through the currently distorted right side of her mouth. He wasn't sure if she saw him or not as he dropped the lumber to the floor and slid the noose around her head.

In the back of his mind, he thought of a house he had once stepped inside with his mother. His mother had wanted to buy the house, but they had not been able to afford it. The much younger version of himself who had been with her had been bummed; there had been a very cool upstairs bedroom he could have done a lot with.

He thought of that room as he cinched the rope tighter. He took a moment to enjoy the panic in Dhayna Tsui's eyes before he set about finishing up his work.

CHAPTER EIGHT

By the time Greg Seamster had been captured, brought in, and released, there were only six addresses left to check over, and Armstrong's men volunteered to knock them out. So far, they were reporting nothing suspicious, other than an apparent rat infestation in one of the homes closer to the lake. A few of them had made it known that they felt as if they were wasting their time. But with a killer on the loose and the FBI in town, they had no real choice but to obey.

Kate and DeMarco meanwhile found themselves once again hunched over the map back in the little conference room, trying to come up with some other approach to locating the killer.

"Sorry about Seamster being a bust," DeMarco said, adding with a smile, "That was hardly worth running across a roof, was it?"

"No. But it was fun, all the same."

"Any ideas? Theories?"

"Maybe one," Kate said. "I'd like to talk to the owners of the properties. And what about contractors? The house Bea Faraday was killed in had been sitting on the market for a while, right? We need to find the owner and/or contractor who worked on the house... and remember, someone was already squatting there, or so it seemed."

"Now that's a good point," DeMarco said.

Kate knew it was a good point, and was honestly a little disappointed that DeMarco had not been able to come up with it on her own. She sorted through the files, looking for the detail sheets on each of the houses. The contractor names weren't on

them, but the phone number and business locations of the builders were. She wasn't too familiar with construction practices, but
knew that the builder and the contractor weren't always one and
the same.

She called the number listed on the sheet for the first house,
but it went straight to voice mail. She left a message and promptly
called the number on the second sheet—the detail listing for the
property on Hammermill Street. This time, the call was answered
after two rings by a bubbly-sounding woman.

"Thanks for calling First Choice Construction. How can I help
you?"

"I'm looking for the name and number of the contractor for
the property at 157 Hammermill Street," Kate said. "And I need the
information urgently, please."

"Can I ask what this is in regards to?" the woman asked. Her
tone indicated that she was well aware that the house in question
might be of particular interest to people with morbid senses of
humor or those wanting to play pranks.

"My name is Kate Wise, and I'm an FBI agent."

She went on to give her badge number and the name of her
direct supervisor. That seemed to do it. She had the name and
number of the contractor—who also happened to be the house's
owner—right away. While she was on a roll, she figured she may as
well try pushing a bit farther.

"I was wondering...could you perhaps get me the information
for another property? Even if it's not one you built. Do you have
some kind of a system for that sort of thing?"

"No, we don't. But it just so happens that the name I just gave
you—Donald Dewalt—owns several properties and plots of land
that other contractors and construction companies have worked
on. It's a long shot, but if you give me the address, I can check to
see if it's on his list of properties."

"That would be great," Kate said. "Thank you."

She was placed on hold as Sheriff Armstrong poked her head
into the office. "I just spoke with Greg's mom. I told her that if she

can't keep him at home, he'll have to spend some time in a holding cell the next time he gets into trouble."

Kate had many thoughts on that, namely that the local PD was being too flexible with the Greg Seamster situation, but she said nothing. Even if she had felt the need to speak it out loud, she would not have had the chance. The woman on the other end picked the line back up and seemed quite proud that she had news to deliver.

"Turns out Mr. Dewalt *does* own that property," she said. "Looks like it's about ten years old and was recently put on the market."

"Yes, that's correct. How many of these properties does Mr. Dewalt own?"

"Well, there are about twenty houses here in Estes, but he owns quite a few rentals out on the lake."

"You've already given me his number," Kate said. "Would you happen to know if he's around anywhere?"

"That I couldn't tell you. But he's always been something of a homebody."

"Do you have a home address?"

"Sure, one second."

As she was placed on hold again, Kate peered over at Armstrong. "You know of a guy named Donald Dewalt?"

"Oh yeah. Big landowner over on the lake. I think he owns upwards of twenty-five percent of the rental properties and runs some of them through a no-name little rental agency. But lately, he's been phasing that out and doing the whole Airbnb thing…making a fortune from what I understand."

"But he's not into construction?"

"No, not that I know of."

Kate considered this for a moment. There was certainly nothing wrong with someone buying up land in an area where the land could then be sold at a profit, improving them and then making bank. But when that ventured into common real estate and two of the properties he owned or contracted on were the recent murder sites, things certainly got much more interesting.

The woman at First Choice Construction came back on the line and gave her the home address for Donald Dewalt. She seemed a bit nervous about giving the information out and ended the call rather quickly.

"So," Kate said, stepping away from the map on the table and plugging the address into her phone. "Looks like we're going to be paying Dewalt a visit. Sheriff Armstrong, do you know anything about him? Is he going to be helpful or a hindrance?"

"Based on what I've heard, you may have to show great restraint to not knock his teeth down his throat."

Kate and DeMarco glanced to one another, sharing a smirk. "Well," DeMarco said, "it's a damned shame neither of us is particularly good with restraint."

CHAPTER NINE

Donald Dewalt lived nearly half an hour outside of Estes. As Kate drove toward the address, she noticed that the route she was taking wound away from the lake at an almost harsh angle. The farther away from the lake they got, the better the houses looked. They passed high-end subdivisions and two golf communities until they reached the even smaller town of Pebble Row.

As far as Kate was concerned, the town was nearly as pretentious as its name. It was small for the sake of being small, populated with homes that overlooked enormous backyards. None were decorated to look beachy, as that sort of style would likely somehow lessen the appeal of the expensive homes. No, these homes were far too good for that staged beach look. If Kate had to venture a guess, she'd place each home in Pebble Row a little north of the million-dollar mark.

It was slightly after five in the afternoon by the time Kate pulled the car into Dewalt's driveway. The home had a long, paved driveway that led to a three-car garage. The door to one of the sections was opened, revealing an expensive speedboat. There was no porch but a gorgeous strip of landscaping running along the front of the house, complete with odd-looking Japanese trees and color-coordinated flowers.

Kate almost felt like some ruthless vagabond as she rang the doorbell. She rolled her eyes at the church-like bell chime that sounded inside. She was sure a house like this had a great security system and felt certain that there was a screen or app or something that allowed those inside to see who was ringing.

It took about twenty seconds before anyone made it to the door. It was answered by a teenage girl, barely even looking at them as she answered. Her head was craned down toward the phone she held in her hand. She looked to be fifteen or sixteen and quite pretty, though it was clear that she was wearing a ton of makeup. Her generous cleavage was on display, hugged tight by a black tank top.

"Yeah?" she asked, her eyes darting between the two women standing in front of her and whatever was currently on the screen of her phone.

"We're looking for Donald Dewalt," Kate said.

The girl briefly looked up at them again and nodded. "That's my dad," she said, as if it pained her to admit it. "Hold on a second."

Without waiting for another word, the girl shut the door in their faces.

"Cute kid," DeMarco said.

They waited on the doorstep, Kate hoping the father was a bit more hospitable than the daughter. When the door was opened again about two minutes later, the man standing in front of them didn't give her much room to hope, though. He was dressed like he had just come off of the golf course. He looked to be in his late fifties. He was ruggedly handsome, his hair having gone a salt-and-pepper shade. The expression on his face when he saw two women at his door was a smug one. It made Kate think he likely got whatever he wanted when it came to women and he was not seeing them as much of a hindrance... other than that they had interrupted his afternoon.

"Who are you?" the man—presumably Donald Dewalt—asked.

Kate was more than happy to show her badge and ID to the glaring man. "We're Agents Wise and DeMarco with the FBI. We'd like to ask you some questions about a few certain properties you own."

"Ah, Jesus," Dewalt said. "I figured this was going to happen."

"And what is that supposed to mean?" DeMarco asked.

"I know about the murders. I figured someone would come to talk to me sooner rather than later."

"Can we come in?" Kate asked.

"Actually, no," he said. "We're about to have dinner and I'd much rather my daughter not hear about what has been happening in my properties in Estes."

He stepped out onto the large front step and glared at them. He crossed his arms and it almost seemed as if he were *trying* to crowd their space. *Yeah,* Kate thought. *He's used to just pushing women around. Not just women, probably.*

"Like I said, we're about to have dinner. My wife is nearly done. You've got five minutes."

Kate wanted very badly to let him know that if it took more than five minutes, they could get that extra time out of him. And it would likely include a few police cars pulling up in front of his fancy-ass house. But she didn't see the point in making the situation more strained than it had to be.

"It seems as if you already know why we're here," Kate said. "The properties at 157 Hammermill and 1806 Leander Drive. You know about the murders?"

"Yes. The real estate companies told me about them."

"So you knew that your properties were the only link between them?" DeMarco asked.

"Link? How's that a link? I own a bunch of properties. It's not all that coincidental that two random murders occurred in two of them."

"In most cases, I'd agree with you," Kate said. "But being that *you* own both of those properties, it's *you* that is the link. It's not even one single real estate company; the properties, as you know, are listed by two different companies."

"Now hold on," Dewalt said. He did not sound nervous or defensive, but irate. "It sounds like you're trying to shove a square into a circular hole. You can't just place me in the middle of your investigation because I own both of those properties. Not only is that a huge stretch, but it makes it seem—to me, at least—that you don't have any idea how to find any answers without throwing wild accusations around carelessly."

"That's not what we're doing," Kate said. "We wanted to know if there was anything about the properties or the agents that you could share with us."

"All I know for sure is that because of these murders, the houses are going to be harder to sell."

"That's very compassionate of you," DeMarco said.

"Well, I'm not a policeman or an FBI agent. My compassion would do nothing. It certainly wouldn't help you find a killer, and it sure as hell isn't going to sell my properties."

"Did you ever have interactions with either of the deceased agents?" Kate asked. This was something of a small trap. She wanted to see how much he had asked, or how much he had been told.

"Yes, I knew Tamara Bateman quite well. She and I have worked together on a few of my lake properties. I was quite upset to hear what had happened to her. I was especially upset because the last… wait, this is none of your concern."

"It is, actually," DeMarco said. She stepped forward and crossed her arms as well, almost as if she were mocking him. "Look, Mr. Dewalt. You've got this gorgeous house, a nice family, tons of properties out on the lake, and I don't doubt there are many people within a fifty-mile radius or so that think you're King Turd of Shit Mountain. Good for you. But that means nothing in the face of the federal government. So either drop the attitude, or we can make this whole thing very long and drawn out. You follow me?"

Kate had to bite at the inside of her bottom lip not to smile at this. DeMarco was a small-statured woman, but when she broke out the bitchy side of her persona, she was like an entirely different person. While it did not make Dewalt flinch in the slightest, his tone was a bit softer when he spoke again.

"Yes, I follow you," he said, basically hissing the words. "And I don't appreciate being threatened."

"Those were not threats. If you fail to answer our questions accurately, we can indeed make this hard for you."

"Fine. I'll answer."

"Good. Now… what were you saying about Ms. Bateman?"

"I was saying that the last time I spoke with Tamara, it did not go so well. The house she was killed in—the one on Hammermill Street—we argued back and forth on the pricing. She said I was asking Pebble Row money for it and I just wasn't going to get it. We had a pretty stern argument right there in the Lakeside Realty offices."

"Do you recall how long ago that was?" Kate asked.

"Two days before she was killed."

"And when was the last time you had stepped foot in the house on Hammermill Street?" DeMarco asked.

"The day I purchased it from the builder. It was a few years old and some of the changes I wanted made to it ... I was being told they could not be made without severe structural damage. I'd say that was about six weeks ago."

"Mr. Dewalt, what about Bea Faraday?" Kate asked. "Did you know her?"

"Not personally. I had seen her face and name on a few real estate ads around Estes and surrounding areas, but no ... I did not know her personally. I don't know that I even ever met her. I did speak to her on the phone several times."

"Did you—" Kate began.

The ringing of DeMarco's phone interrupted her. She glanced at it quickly, seemed to consider whether or not to answer it, and then stepped away from Kate and Dewalt. As DeMarco took the call, Kate went on with her questions.

"Have you ever had issues with squatters in your properties?" Kate asked.

"No, not squatters. There was one time a year or so ago where some kids shacked up in one of my rental properties over the course of a week or so in the winter but that was it. Cops checked it out and said they thought some sort of big party took place. I'm sure there have been other instances of it, but if so, no one was ever caught. Why do you ask?"

Before she could answer, DeMarco spoke her name.

"Kate, we have to roll. There's been a third murder back in Estes."

"How recent?" Kate asked.

"Very." DeMarco leaned in a bit, making sure Dewalt could not hear her. "Armstrong says there's blood everywhere."

With nothing more than a muttered thank you and a wave goodbye, Kate and DeMarco turned away from Dewalt and headed back to their car. Kate noticed that Dewalt was still standing by his front door, as if confused, while they pulled away from his house and pointed the car back toward Estes.

CHAPTER TEN

When Kate pulled the car in front of the house Armstrong had given them the address for, she saw two cops and a man dressed in a button-down shirt and jeans standing on the front porch steps. One of the cops was Armstrong. Kate was pretty sure the other was the young man Armstrong had called Jimmy.

The house looked to be relatively new, located expertly on the side of a cul-de-sac that, like the house, looked unblemished. The street was Magnolia Street, a name that seemed almost too perfect and innocent as far as Kate was concerned. Kate wasn't sure why, exactly, but the idea of murder and blood in a place this fresh and vivid felt weird and almost obscene.

They approached Armstrong, Jimmy, and the other man. The man looked a bit dazed, looking blankly at Armstrong.

"Agents," Armstrong said, "this is Travis Fields. He's the supervisor for a small lighting company out of Estes. He came in a little less than an hour ago to take measurements for a space in the kitchen for recessed lights and found the victim."

"It's bad," was all he said. "Never seen anything like that."

"Have *you* been inside?" Kate asked Armstrong.

She nodded, nibbling at the corner of a frown. "Yeah. And he's not exaggerating. It's pretty bad. I knew the victim, though not well. A young Asian woman named Dhayna Tsui."

Kate was anxious to go in but couldn't leave Travis Fields so soon after the discovery. "Did you see anyone else in the area when you arrived?" she asked.

"Just a kid over there in the yard," Fields said, nodding to a big white house two yards over, at the very edge of where the cul-de-sac started to become a circle. "Scribbling on his sidewalk with chalk. If there was anyone else out here, I didn't see them."

"Did you examine the house once you found the body or did you come right outside?"

Fields let out a nervous chuckle here, one that sounded a little close to the edge of madness for Kate's liking. "I sort of froze, you know? Staring at her. My brain just sort of locked up before it started screaming at me to call the police. I'd say it took five or six seconds before I hauled ass back out here. Went to my truck right there," he said, nodding to the black work truck parked on the edge of the street. "Damn near started crying before I was able to finally call the police."

"Was this the first time you'd been inside the house?"

"No. When it was originally built three years ago, I did all of the lighting."

"That was the last time you'd been inside?"

"Yes."

"How much time would you say passed between your discovery of the body and placing the call?" DeMarco asked.

"Maybe two minutes. Probably less."

"Thank you, Mr. Fields," Kate said. "Would you mind hanging around just a bit longer while we check the place over? And Sheriff Armstrong ... see if you can find out who the previous owner is."

"Well hell, I know that myself," Fields said. "It's one of Governor Moore's houses. He's been trying to sell it for about six weeks."

"As in the governor of the state?" Kate asked.

"Yeah. From what I hear, he's been trying to sell it privately for a few months but it just wouldn't go for the price he was looking for. So he hired Crest Realty to try to move it for him."

Two homes belonging to a wealthy local and now one belonging to the governor of the state of Delaware, Kate thought. *This might be much deeper than just random murders in nice homes ...*

With an uneasy feeling building in her stomach, Kate walked up the sidewalk and to the front door. As she reached for the doorknob, she saw that it hadn't been closed all the way. And in the small crack between the door and the frame, she could already see blood on the floor. A lot of it.

She pushed the door open, DeMarco falling in right beside her. They stepped in one right behind the other and froze in place almost at the exact same time.

"My God," DeMarco said.

Kate only nodded in agreement. What they were looking at was indeed quite grisly, but she was both blessed and cursed to have endured a career that had offered up much worse.

Dhayna Tsui had gotten an almost identical treatment as Tamara Bateman. She had been strung up from the stairs, hanging from the very top. The rope was tied around the thick wood rail, her body dangling in the air directly against the side of the wall beneath the stairs. The entire left side of her face was a sheet of blood. The top portion of her head looked misshapen, a clear indication of a massive skull fracture.

Blood had run down onto her light blue shirt, most of it soaking in to make a very large dark red stain that was nearly black. More if it ran down her arm, dripping from her fingers where it either smeared along the walls or dropped down to the floor like red rain. It reminded Kate of what Mary Seibert had said about the Bea Faraday scene: "... *that's the thing that keeps me from sleeping at night. It's not the poor woman's face or even the gross scene itself; it's the sound that fresh blood made when it splattered on the floor—that dripping sound.*"

The gruesome sight of Dhayna Tsui was so bad that it took Kate roughly five seconds to notice the other abnormal thing sticking out in plain sight. Above them, a large light fixture hung from the ceiling. It was not quite a chandelier but a modern, industrial-looking light with four large arms holding light globes. One of the arms was broken, its metallic arm dangling only by the cord that ran to the light itself. Also, the base of the light was slightly jarred from the ceiling. It sat crooked, slightly bent and hanging down just enough to be noticeable.

"What do you think of that?" Kate asked, nodding up to the light.

"Not sure. Wasn't the electrician here for lights? Maybe he was going to fix that."

"He said he was here for checking on space for recessed lights. I think he would have mentioned needing to fix something like that."

"Maybe the killer got overzealous," DeMarco suggested. "Wanted to see if he could recreate the Bea Faraday scene."

"There's no way he could have made that toss," Kate said. She pointed from the light to the stairs, where Dhayna hung. "That's at least ten feet. Maybe twelve. I think he tried to hang her from the light but she was too heavy, or his force on the rope was too much."

They both looked directly in front of them. There was a large pool of blood, still wet and smeared, to support this. Kate walked to the stairs and climbed them with caution and respect. She reached the body and examined the rope. It was wrapped around the rail several times. She could not measure it without unraveling it, which she did not want to do as that was a chore for forensics, but she felt positive it would have been long enough to throw one end up over the light. Then, with the other end tied around Dhayna's throat, the killer would have pulled, trying to get her in the air.

But the arm on the chandelier had broken. Of course it had. Anyone with common sense would have suspected it would happen. She wondered if that meant the killer wasn't the brightest of individuals or if he had just gotten caught up in the heat of the kill. She knew that some killers tended to go into a fugue state when carrying out their acts.

"The blood trail stretches around the stairs," DeMarco pointed out.

She was inching toward the large entrance on the left side of the stairs. Kate joined her, walking through a large living space and then into an equally large kitchen. A trail of blood worked its way through it all, as if her body had been dragged from the kitchen to the stairs. There was a considerable amount of blood on the kitchen floor. A huge pool of it sat two feet away from the kitchen counter. There were splatter marks on the counter itself, and even a few on the far wall, over the sink.

"He struck her with something hard," Kate said, taking in the scene. "And he put some considerable strength behind it."

"I'll make a note for the coroner to come up with some ideas of what the weapon might have been," DeMarco said. "If we compare it to the condition of the other two victims, we could maybe get an idea of what weapon the killer is using."

"That could be a smoking gun, actually," Kate said, liking the idea. "The state of Dhayna Tsui's head is fairly similar to what we saw on Tamara Bateman."

"Wise, this guy is a maniac. We have to find him."

It was an obvious statement, but that made it no less true. All murders were obviously bad. But when done with this degree of violence, it made the whole matter seem all the more urgent. It also usually indicated that the killer had no real schedule or agenda. He'd kill again if given the chance, and it could be very soon.

"Agents?"

The voice was soft and respectful—that of Sheriff Armstrong, coming from the front door. Kate and DeMarco returned to the front of the house, where Armstrong had stepped inside but seemed to be doing everything she could to not look directly at the body hanging in front of them.

"Sorry to interrupt, but I had to call the State Police on this one. Something like this happens in one of the governor's homes—*especially* one he's trying to sell—and we have to let him know. He's already called me. I just got off the phone with him. He's nervous as hell."

"Nervous about what?"

"He's nervous what the story is going to look like. A woman murdered in a home he had been trying to get rid of for almost two months. It will raise questions... dumb ones, but the kind that make great headlines. He wouldn't admit to it, but I'm assuming he has some money tied up in questionable real estate ventures. And this is the last thing he needs. I know it's all shitty politics, but still... that's where we are right now."

Oh, I'm used to politics, Kate thought. But honestly, she couldn't care less what sort of nervousness the governor might be feeling. She was more worried about the family and friends of Dhayna Tsui. She was even more worried about the other real estate agents in Estes and the surrounding areas.

"Sheriff, I know it's not going to make you a popular woman," Kate said, "but as of this moment, I think it's for the best if we put a freeze on all real estate showings and transactions."

"I was thinking the same thing but... well, it seems drastic. And right now, coming off of the summer, I'm going to get a hell of a lot of pushback."

"Let them push, then," Kate said. "And if they have any major complaints, you can send them to me."

It sounded overly tough, but she didn't care. Looking up at the misshapen and bloody face of Dhayna Tsui, she felt the need to do or say just about anything to feel some semblance of hope and control.

CHAPTER ELEVEN

Forensics came and went, Armstrong notified Dhayna's family, and night settled down on the coast. Kate discovered she had been correct; there had been more than enough rope to attempt throwing it over the arms of the light fixture and attempting to hang Dhayna that way. Once a ladder had been brought in and the light was looked over, rope fibers had been found on the iron material of the light, proving Kate's theory.

Kate and DeMarco looked the house over for any signs of a squatter but found none. They even canvassed the neighborhood with the help of Armstrong and a few of her officers, but no one had seen anyone or anything suspicious in the neighborhood all afternoon.

With no answers in sight and the only hope coming in the assurances from forensics and the coroner that something would eventually turn up, Kate and DeMarco checked into a hotel. It was the same hotel DeMarco had stayed at the night before. It was close enough to the lake that they could hear the buzzing of boat engines just outside the building, but could not see the water.

Because DeMarco had already checked into a room the night before, Kate got her own room. The two said good night right away, though Kate felt an uncharacteristic draw to go to the bar just across the street. It had been a long, stressful day, and she could go for a glass of wine. But she fought the urge and went straight to her room. There, she checked her phone and saw that she had a missed call and two texts from Allen. They came as no surprise; she had seen and heard them coming in all afternoon.

The first message read: **I know your work is important. Just once, though, I'd like to share mine with you. If we're going to remain together, this trip could be important for both of us.**

The message did not make her angry or upset in any way. She was actually indifferent to it. She knew she could be quite selfish when it came to work. Allen knew it, too. And he usually took it like a champ. But now, especially after the last case and the time they had spent together afterward, things were different. They were closer now. There was something more between them. Love … sure. But something else, too. Something else that made Kate think about the rest of her life.

The second text read: **Here's the deal. Meeting went very well. Headed out for drinks in a bit. Plan on getting toasted. Want to talk to you, but maybe we do our own thing tonight. If I get truly toasted, maybe you'll get a mushy phone call or a weird selfie from me. Take care.**

One thing she had learned about Allen was that when he got wordy in texts or said a lot of "like" or "um" in conversation, he was hiding his true feelings. So what those two texts told her was that there would likely be some damage control to handle when she got back home.

Kate changed into her pajama pants and a T-shirt before settling into bed. She was tired, but did not think she'd be able to go to sleep right away. She ended up being right. She spent too much time thinking about the crime scenes and the victims. She felt there were a lot of clues hiding in plain sight—connections that maybe weren't solid but were heavily implied.

After a while, she looked at the bedside clock and saw that it was 11:20. She sighed, sat up, and said: "To hell with it."

She kept the T-shirt on but slipped into her jeans—the only other pants she had packed other than what she had worn that day. She grabbed the car keys, which DeMarco had gladly allowed her to keep, and headed back down to the lobby. Kate stepped out into the night, got into the car, and headed east.

It took less than two minutes to reach the last row of motels and houses before she came to the edge of the lake. She found a public access parking lot, parked, and got out. Smiling like a little girl, she kicked her shoes off as she neared the access pier that led down to the soft sand that bordered the lake. It was a far cry from the beach trip she and Allen had taken, but she was a firm believer that sand between the toes—be it from a lake or a beach—was some weird form of therapy.

She took a few steps out into the sand, relishing the feel of it on her feet. She sat down on the sand, looking into the sheet of darkness stretched out over the lake. Her mind wanted to drift to romantic and uplifting things—perhaps sharing this moment with Allen, or wondering how old Michelle would be when Melissa finally took her to a lake or ocean or body of water other than the YMCA pool.

But her mind was too focused on the case. All her mind could center on as she stared out into that darkness was trying to come up with some sort of a profile for their killer.

The fact that he was hanging the women spoke volumes about him. This was not going to be a timid man. This would be a killer who put thought into what he was doing. Maybe he didn't necessarily take pride in it, but he needed it to be a display of some sort rather than a simple murder. History and academy studies told her that killers who put some element of the dramatic or artistic in their work usually had some sort of trauma or emotional scarring in their past. And emotional killers tended to be the most dangerous. Logic and reasoning became just shadows in a world that was littered with reasons to kill.

She also assumed the killer didn't know the women personally. The fact that each victim had been a real estate agent meant that he was choosing them because of their profession. One or two could be passed off as a coincidence, but *three* pointed toward the victims being purposefully chosen. She wondered if the killer had been homeless at some point in his life or if he was acting out against people who worked to purchase larger, more expensive homes.

One of the first things Kate had wondered after seeing the first crime scene and hearing the report details was that the killer could possibly be someone from another real estate agency. But now that they had a dead agent from each of three local real estate agencies in the area, that theory was effectively ruled out.

It had also played out that the same-owner theory had fallen through. Had Donald Dewalt owned the house that Dhayna Tsui had been killed in, that would have obviously been a clear link, providing them somewhere to dig. But now Kate felt as if they were starting over at square one. She ran over the things she felt certain of in her mind, each item punctuated by a crashing wave in front of her. She checked each one off in her mind, creating a list and trying to tie it to a profile.

He's a local because he's familiar with the real estate agencies and current listings.

He's attacking the women with something hard, hitting them in the head and then hanging them in foyer areas, as close to the front of the house as he can.

He's not afraid to attack in the middle of the day, in broad daylight; that likely means he's not feeling guilt or shame for what he is doing.

So far, he's only gone after female agents.

It was a scant list, but it was better than nothing. And the more Kate let it sink in, the more she thought something there might be able to lead them in the right direction.

First and foremost, it made her think of the easy access to the home. The killer was having no problem getting into these homes, which made Kate think of the electrician, poor Travis Fields. It made her wonder what other sorts of people had access to the houses at the same times they were being shown to potential buyers.

It also made her wonder if any potential buyers had visited all three homes. And if so, had they stuck with one agency or had they shopped around to all three?

Once she started picking at that thread, she felt like it could unravel on and on forever. And when you were looking for the answers to some very hard questions, an unraveling thread could be a very good thing.

She wasn't sure how long she sat in the sand, peering into the darkness and watching the murky movements of the water, but when she stood to her feet and glanced at her watch, it was 12:16. She brushed the sand from her backside as she headed back to the walkway. She gave the dark water one last glance and continued on to the parking lot.

The following morning, Kate and DeMarco showed up at the offices of Lakeside Realty as soon as the doors opened. When Brett Towers arrived and unlocked the door, he didn't bother hiding the frown that crept across his face.

"It's early," he complained as he opened the door. Still, ever the gentleman, he held the door open for Kate and DeMarco as they entered the office.

"I know," Kate said. "But we only have a few questions…just a few bits of information we were hoping you could help us with. I assume you've heard the news about Dhayna Tsui?"

"I have. And I've also heard about how you think it's necessary to essentially take money out of my pocket by putting a freeze on all real estate showings until this is all over with."

"That's true," Kate said. "So the quicker we wrap it, the sooner you can get back to work. So if you could help us gather up some of this information, you'd be helping to push things along."

They followed him to his desk in the back of the large open office area. He plopped down in his chair and turned on his laptop. "What sort of information are you looking for?" he asked.

"I need the names and professions of anyone who was allowed into the house on Hammermill Street in the week or so prior to Tamara Bateman's death. Painters, electricians, cleaners, other agents, everything you can get me."

"That should actually be fairly simple. I'll have to check the records, but I can have it for you pretty quickly."

"How's the whole thing work?" DeMarco asked. "If one agency has the property listed, another one can't show it, too, right?"

"Yeah. Unless there's some weird segregation of the house itself and the property it sits on."

"So in other words," Kate said, wanting to clarify, "because Lakeside has the house on Hammermill listed, Crest Realty or Davis and Hopper can't show it?"

"That's right. Once a seller signs with one agency, they can only list it with another agency once that contract expires, or if there is due cause for them to terminate."

He began hunting around in his laptop, moving with expert speed. He started to nod as he clicked along. "Yeah, there's quite a few names here that I can send you. I've got three people who saw the house with us, then one electrician, a carpet guy that went in for an estimate, the county appraiser … yeah, it's a long list."

"Is that normal?" Kate asked.

"Yeah. I mean, if there was damage to a house, the list could be *very* long. Painters, carpenters, gutter installers, you name it. The Hammermill house was in good shape, though. All things considered, this list isn't anything out of the ordinary."

"Thanks, Mr. Towers," DeMarco said. "We'll leave you alone for now. You think you could compile that list and text it to me?"

"Sure thing. Give me about ten more minutes."

Kate and DeMarco took their leave. Even though it was still early, Kate felt that the day was going to be a busy one. But that was fine with Kate. She'd much rather have an overwhelming list of potential leads than no direction whatsoever. She felt a stirring of excitement with the possibilities. If the other two agencies could provide lists the size and scope of the one Brett Towers was putting together for them, they might have their work cut out for them.

CHAPTER TWELVE

He sipped from his coffee, watching the house from behind the steering wheel. It was a stunning morning, the sun bright but not too hot. It shone down on the casual little neighborhood as if it were the spotlight from a play, the lighting crew bringing this one little block into the light. He grinned as he watched the door open.

The woman who came out was very pretty. Her blonde hair was pulled back into a loose ponytail. She had a face that could have been on TV and a body that could have been in any number of men's magazines. Out of the ones he had been following so far, she was easily the prettiest. He wasn't sure how old she was. Surely no older than forty.

As he watched the house, a man came out behind her. He said something—he could not tell what because he was parked four houses down—and chased after her. The woman smiled, turned around, and wrapped her arms around him. The kiss they then shared was a bit much out in the front yard on a weekday morning. Still, he smiled. It was a kiss that made him think the couple he was currently watching might have quite a fun afternoon when she arrived back home.

The kiss broke and when the woman turned away and headed for her car, the man slapped her playfully on her perfectly sculpted backside. Behind the steering wheel, coffee in hand, he continued smiling. It was a whimsical little scene, a great way to start the day, he supposed.

He wondered if his parents had ever enjoyed one another in such a way. He barely remembered his father, and what he *did* remember was not good. But whenever his mother had spoken about his father, she would sort of light up. She would never admit that she missed him and he only once heard her say that she had loved his father, but he hoped they had shared some days like the one this couple was currently having.

The smile on his face felt odd. It was the first time he had not felt sad or filled with pain when thinking of his mother ever since her funeral. There was still a sting behind the thought of her, but it was almost numb now. It almost made sense. By God, he missed her.

He missed how hard she had fought for them, trying to make sure he had the best possible future. He missed her optimism, although it had been annoying as hell at times.

This terrible world had not treated her fairly. And none of it had been her fault. Most of it had come down to his father leaving, but the rest had been circumstantial. It had come down to a world that simply did not look favorably on people like his mother—people who had been dealt a shitty hand and tried to make do any way they possibly could.

He was so sidetracked by thoughts of his mother that he nearly zoned out and missed the woman getting into her car and pulling away from the sidewalk. He let her get to the end of the block before he pulled out into the street. Really, though, he wasn't too worried about keeping her in his sights. He knew where she was headed.

What he was more interested in was where she might be going later in the day.

He wondered if she would be showing houses today. He wondered if she'd have to be alone in any of them for some reason or another.

As he took the same right turn she had taken just moments ago, he heard the piece of lumber jostle under his seat as if it, too, was anxious to know about the rest of her day.

CHAPTER THIRTEEN

While Kate knew that her request to put a hold on all real estate showings was not a popular one, the agencies still seemed more than willing to assist her. By the time she and DeMarco arrived at the Estes police station, Davis and Hopper Realty had also compiled a list of people who had been given access to the property on Leander Drive a week leading up to Bea Faraday's murder. DeMarco copied and pasted the names into the Notes app on her phone and printed it out from one of the station's' printer. While she was doing this, Kate revisited the map in the conference room and, with Sheriff Armstrong's assistance, placed a third X in the vicinity of the murders.

Kate studied the layout of streets and landmarks among the three X's but could still see no discernable pattern. She felt that looking for a pattern might be wasted time but because it was such a small area, it had to be considered. Sure, she and DeMarco—along with the help of some of Estes's finest—had searched the houses of interest yesterday and come up with no signs of a squatter or any traces of forced entry. But still, there had to be *something* she was missing.

DeMarco came back into the room with the list of names to look over. She placed it on the edge of the table with a bit of flair, sighed, and crossed her arms. "This is a long list," she said. "But I've already noticed that there are some duplicate entries. For instance, the same carpet company works for both agencies."

"Still no list from Crest Realty?" Kate asked.

"None."

"They aren't exactly known for their promptness," Armstrong said. "We may have to press a bit harder to get anything from them."

"Well, we may as well start on the list then," Kate said. She did not like the idea of spending the entire morning on the phone, but it had to be done.

"Hey, wait a second," DeMarco said. She was looking at the map again, from an angle at the edge of the table. "Sheriff Armstrong...what's this little area here?"

She was pointing to an expanse of land that sat to the right of the Leander Drive property and just above the Hammermill house. The third house, the latest one on the cul-de-sac on Magnolia Street and marked with a fresh X, sat on the other side of that expanse of land.

"Locals call it Old Park Place," Armstrong said. "There was a little park there for the longest time. I remember playing on it when I was a kid. A playground, a little garden space, and even a little pond. Look real hard on the map and you can see the pond."

"But it's no longer open?" DeMarco said.

"No. It closed down seven or eight years ago. The sad truth is, there's just not a lot of kids in the community. And during the summer, ninety percent of the children in the area are more interested in heading to the lake. It wasn't worth the cost and management to keep it up, so it was closed down and sort of went to ruin. Every now and then we'll catch people drinking out there. Some kids necking from time to time. Our buddy Greg Seamster has been known to sleep there on occasion."

"When it was opened, were there trails and roads inside of it?" DeMarco asked.

Kate knew where DeMarco was headed with her questions and admired her for it. It might be a bit of a stretch, but then again it might also help them find that pattern she had been looking for.

"There were, yes. There's a thin road that would barely be considered a two-lane that ran along the southern edge of it. It wasn't even marked. And there's a little nature trail that curved around the pond..."

It was then that Armstrong also seemed to understand what DeMarco was getting at. They all looked at the map together, bending over in unison. To anyone who might randomly walk by the opened conference room door, the sight may have been comical.

No one said anything because it had become obvious they were all saying the same thing. Kate nearly did but she wanted to give DeMarco the opportunity to see this hunch through. When she *did* pick it up, there was the slightest bit of excitement in her voice.

"So on this map, there are no clearly defined roads or passages in and out of this chunk of land. But to someone passing through the area on foot, it could serve to connect a few of the nearby streets—sort of like a shortcut of kids were out walking or riding skateboards and bikes."

"That's right," Armstrong agreed. "I actually believe that some of the town maintenance crews use it as a kind of thoroughfare when they need to get a lot of work done in a short period of time."

"And when you look at this Old Park Place as a potential connecting point to these surrounding streets, the latest crime scene really doesn't seem all that far away from the Leander Drive scene."

She was right. When Old Park Place looked to be nothing more than a blank scrap of land and forest, the two properties were a considerable distance away from one another—three miles at least. But if Old Park Place could be used as a shortcut between the two, Kate estimated the trip might be barely over a mile. This line of thinking put all three crime scenes within about two and a half square miles of one another.

"So what does it mean?" Armstrong asked.

"Maybe nothing," DeMarco said.

"But it could mean that the killer used it as a shortcut *and* a hiding spot," Kate said. She figured even if the hunch came to nothing, she wanted DeMarco to realize that the idea had been wholly hers and that it was a credible thought. DeMarco looked back to her with a grin, having understood this. "If he was squatting in these homes, he'd need some way to get between them without being seen…some way to escape quickly, right?"

"Makes sense to me," DeMarco said.

"It's still early," Kate said. "Maybe if we can canvass the neighborhoods around Old Park Place and the streets the murders occurred on, someone will know something. Three murders in such a small amount of time makes me think it would be next to impossible for the killer to not have been seen by *someone*. Especially if he was going in and out of an old overgrown park."

"While you two get on that," Armstrong said, picking up the list of names and contact information DeMarco had brought in, "my team and I will start running through this list."

Kate could hear disappointment in the sheriff's voice. She was apparently very much like Kate; she did not relish the idea of spending her morning on the phone.

"You know, maybe you can just let your team run with it," Kate said. "We've got a lot of ground and houses to cover. It might do us good to have not only another set of feet, but a set of feet that knows the area well."

Armstrong did her best to hide the appreciation and excitement in her expression as she instantly started for the door. "I can do that," she said. "Let me get my men on task, and I'll meet you out front."

When she was out of the room, DeMarco wasted little time. "Thank you for that," she said.

"For what?"

"Letting me run with it. You've been great about making sure you let me know this case is still mine without saying so. I appreciate it."

"Not a problem at all. Good thinking with this Old Park Place idea. I think there could potentially be something to it."

They left the room, leaving the map behind them. Before exiting completely, Kate looked back at the map, staring down at those three X marks. She could only hope that the next time they entered this room, they would not be placing a fourth one on there.

They started at Old Park Place. They had all piled into Armstrong's police cruiser, a strange but somewhat relaxing experience for Kate. It was nice to not have to drive down unfamiliar streets, to have someone maneuvering the town who knew it well. Armstrong parked the car in the old parking lot. Not much had been done to keep intruders out of the abandoned park. There were a few concrete barriers and orange barrels, and that was it. All of it had been set up several yards into the park's entrance, making sure the eyesores could not be seen from the street.

Armstrong had described the place perfectly. The playground had gone to ruin, almost every single swing hanging from rusted chains. The rungs on the sliding board were warped and broken, and wild grass and weeds covered the seesaws and tiled hopscotch field. The pond she had mentioned was visible from the tall grass. It was quite small and almost completely overshadowed by a strip of forest.

"The little connector road to Jackson Street is right over there," Armstrong said, pointing in the opposite direction of the pond. "Where it comes out, there's about half a mile before you come to the road where Dhayna Tsui was killed."

"What about the nature trails?" Kate asked.

"The one around the pond just circles back around and comes out on the other end of the park. But I think there's one stretch of it that comes pretty close to breaking out of the forest. At one point, you can actually catch glimpses of some of the backyards along Colton Street, which intersects with Hammermill a little further up."

"So this truly would be a core of sorts, then," DeMarco said.

"Looks that way," Kate agreed. She then looked to Armstrong and shrugged. "You know the town best. What's our best play here?"

"I say we split up. Someone take the little connector road out to Jackson Street, someone head over to Colton, and the other can pound the pavement on Leander Drive."

The discussion was brief, and Kate ended up taking the nature trail that skirted along Colton Street. She felt a little silly at first, leaving her partner and the local sheriff behind as she traipsed into the forest. The nature trail had grown thin, overtaken by grass and fallen woodland debris. As she walked along, she looked for any signs of recent passage but saw nothing glaringly obvious—just some litter here and there.

After walking along it for no more than a quarter of a mile, she came to the section of the trail Armstrong had mentioned. She could indeed see brief glimpses of backyards through what amounted to about thirty feet or so of scraggly forest. When she found what looked to be the easiest section to cross through, she marched off of the trail and through the little stretch of forest. She came out in a backyard that was blocked off from the woods by a wooden gate. She walked alongside it until she came to the edge and then turned, heading up toward the house.

She knocked at the door of this house. A few knocks and a ringing of the doorbell provided no answer, so she went on to the next, and the next. She didn't get an answer until the fourth house. It was an old gentleman, the morning news blaring from a TV as he spoke to her in his doorway. He did not invite her in, said he had not seen anyone suspicious, and seemed very grateful when she informed him that he should be on the lookout for unfamiliar people walking the streets of his neighborhood.

As she left him behind, she couldn't help but think: *Really? Is this why I didn't go to Chicago with Allen? Is this why Allen is currently pissed at me?*

It was easy to think those things as she went from door to door, hoping for an answer of some kind. But her mind would then bring visions of the three dead real estate agents. She'd see the terrible condition of Dhayna Tsui's head and face and remind herself *that* was why she was not with Allen in Chicago.

And that made it a little easier as she continued to knock on doors, knowing that there was a killer somewhere in this town ... and that he could be doing just about anything while she was going door to door.

❧ ❧ ❧

The first helpful person she spoke to that morning was a middle-aged woman who had been sitting on her porch. It was the fifth person Kate had spoken to, and when the woman offered Kate a coffee, she graciously accepted. The coffee was weak, but it did its job in perking her up a bit.

"You say you're looking for someone I might think looked out of place or suspicious," the woman said. She had introduced herself as Shelly Abercrombie before offering the coffee, and she had also looked slightly concerned that the FBI was in her quaint little town. She looked that way again as she watched Kate nod at her question.

"Yes, that's right. Preferably in the past week or so."

"Well, that's easy. There was a screaming match right there at the end of the street." Shelly pointed to the right, toward the end of the block, with the same hand that was holding her large cup of coffee.

"What was the screaming about?" Kate asked.

"It was Regina again. Regina Voss. She's a grumpy old fart that doesn't really get along with anyone. Lives a few streets over and is always walking her dog. I swear she walks that damned thing five times a day. She was screaming at some young couple—a couple not from around here, I don't think. And there are usually a few of those kinds of couples here in Estes during the summer, as you can imagine."

"Do you know what she was yelling *about*?"

"No, I didn't catch it all. But I can almost guarantee you it was for something stupid. They were probably looking at her the wrong way or something ridiculous like that."

"And that's common for her?"

"Pretty common. But no one takes Regina Voss very seriously. She's just a little crazy, you know? Sort of off the rails, if you ask me. Can't blame her, I guess. Her first husband died at a young age and her second husband left her for a twenty-two-year-old from out of town."

Kate knew better than to believe every word from a bored-looking woman in a small town. But she also knew that most gossip started with a kernel of truth.

"Has Regina Voss always lived in Estes?"

"Been here as long as I have, and I've been here for twenty-three years."

"Do you happen to know where she lives?"

"Sure do. She's just two streets over, on Laurel Street. I don't know the address, but it's the house with all those godawful wind chimes on the front porch. You can't miss it."

"What are the chances she's at home right now?" Kate asked. "Any idea?"

"I'd say pretty good. She doesn't work ... not really. Some online stuff, I think. God only knows what, though. She's either home or walking that stupid dog."

"Thank you for your time, Mrs. Abercrombie."

"Oh, sure," she said. There was a look on her face that made it clear she had plenty more ammunition, should Kate needed it.

But Kate decided not to waste any more time hearing stories from a woman who clearly loved to dole out the gossip. Instead, she walked two streets over and grinned when, as she stopped at the corner and tried to decide which way to go, heard the sound of wind chimes. She nearly started in that direction, but that's when her eyes were drawn across the street.

She was standing at a four-way intersection. Across the road and about a block farther back, there was a property for sale. The bright red and white sign stood out even from where she was standing. Because the street went back at a slight curb, she could see roughly half of the house from its right side. It was a gorgeous home, not quite as big as the ones they had visited so far, but very close. Of course, it might have only appeared that way from the angle she was viewing it from.

Deciding to take chance, Kate crossed the road and headed for the house. It wasn't too much of stretch because it was, after all, located in the area they had singled out as the killer's field of play.

As she neared the house, she noted that there were fewer cars on the street along this stretch of road. She assumed it was because all of the homes she walked by had two-car garages attached to either the fronts or the sides of the homes. The only cars were a single work truck a few houses farther down from the house she was interested in and a lone black Ford Taurus. The Taurus was parked across the street from the house. From what she could tell, the driver was looking directly at the For Sale sign.

The Taurus was an older model, easily ten or twelve years old. It had a few dings and scratches, looking rather out of place within the neighborhood. Kate knew this likely meant nothing; as stereotypical as it made her feel, she knew full well that many people who were hired hands of electricians and carpenters drove beater cars and trucks to their worksites. Still, given the details to the case, she figured it was at least looking into.

Kate slowed her approach as she neared the car. She saw that all of the windows were rolled down to allow some of the cool lake air into the car. The engine was not running, meaning there was no AC.

"Excuse me," Kate said as she came up next to the driver's side door.

The man sitting behind the wheel jumped a bit. He looked irritated and then, when he saw the woman standing next to his car, he gave her a shaky smile. His cheeks were red with embarrassment. "Jesus, lady," he said. "I don't mind telling you, you scared the crap out of me."

"I'm sorry about that," Kate said. "Listen, I was wondering if you were working on something inside of this house."

"That one?" the man asked, nodding toward the larger one with the FOR SALE sign in the yard.

"Yes, that one."

"No. Why do you ask?"

"You were just sort of randomly parked here. And I don't know if you know, but there has been a string of murders in the area."

"I had heard about that," he said. "And no...I'm not doing any work. I just sort of...well, I like to look at these nicer homes. Makes me think of ways to improve myself...my future. Gets me motivated."

"Can you—"

Before she could answer, she was interrupted by the sounds of a woman screaming. It was not a scream of pain or panic, but one of anger. It was coming from behind her and somewhere to the right. She was rather disappointed in herself to find that it was coming from the direction of the house with all of the wind chimes—the house she had been heading to before becoming distracted by the house for sale and the man in the black Taurus. She looked back to the man in the car with an almost apologetic smile. He looked confused, staring at her as if he wasn't sure how to respond to her.

From behind her and just around the corner, she heard the sounds of commotion again. This time there were two voices, and they were escalating in noise and pitch.

"Ma'am, are you okay?" the man asked.

"Yes, I'm fine. You just...look, don't hang around too long." Apparently, he had not yet heard the sounds of the argument carried on the afternoon air.

"Sure," he said.

Kate gave him a final look, deciding that he was harmless. Sure, she'd scared him out of surprise, but he genuinely did not look as if he was trying to hide anything.

"Anything else?" the man asked.

"Nothing," she said, feeling foolish for the fact that she was about to jump to conclusions about this man, casually parked on the side of the road. "Sorry to have bothered you."

"No worries," the man said. "My heart rate is almost back to normal."

Kate gave him a quick smile and then went off running in the other direction, back the way she had come. Step by step, the sounds of people arguing got more heated. She wasn't sure, but she thought she heard a third voice mixed in now, this one a bit lower.

When she reached the intersection, she glanced back at the man in the car one more time. He was no longer looking at the house. He seemed to be looking over into the passenger's seat, like he was looking for something.

By the time Kate was heading to the right and crossing the street, Kate had put the man in the black Taurus out of her mind. She was instead focused on the three women standing on the sidewalk, grouped tightly together. One of them was screaming, the other looked a little scared, and the third, Kate was shocked to find, was DeMarco.

The man in the black Ford Taurus watched the strange woman dash back down the street to the four-way intersection. He didn't like the look of her, and it wasn't just because she had scared the hell out of him by sneaking up on him. She made him feel uneasy—like she was there on purpose.

Like she knew.

It made him nervous. He looked to the floorboard of the passenger's side of the car. Even though none of the blood-soaked piece of lumber showed from beneath the seat, he reached over and slid it a little further under anyway.

Just in case.

Chapter Fourteen

As Kate got closer to the trio of women, it also became clear that it was taking place directly in front of the house she had originally been headed for. The house was a very nice one, with a wraparound porch complete with a porch swing And, as Shelly Abercrombie had indicated, there were quite a few wind chimes on the porch hanging from the rafters. Not cute ones, either. These were gaudy relics from swap meets and yard sales, wind chimes that looked almost comical. They chimed together as Kate approached the scene, their noise quiet but somehow spine-chilling.

As Kate neared the commotion, DeMarco spotted her She gave Kate a look with wide, exaggerated eyes, wordlessly saying: *Oh, thank God you're here.*

The two women were on either side of DeMarco as she tried to keep them apart. The woman doing all of the talking looked to be in her early fifties, maybe a bit younger. The other was probably forty but was wearing the sort of running garb that she probably thought made her look thirty. She also wore a relatively tight top with a low U-collar that reminded her of Donald Dewalt's teenage daughter.

Using the information Shelly Abercrombie had given her, Kate assumed the fifty-something to be Regina Voss. The fact that she was absolutely railing against the younger woman further solidified Shelly Abercrombie's claims.

"...and don't even try this shit of how much you love this town, honey, because I was here long before you! So the next time you want to stick your nose where it don't belong—"

"Whoa," Kate said, stepping in next to DeMarco and throwing up a hand almost as a shield against Regina Voss. "Let's just back up and clam down."

"And who the fuck are you?" Regina Voss asked.

"Agent Kate Wise, Agent DeMarco's partner. And if you keep that tone with either myself, Agent DeMarco, or this other woman, this situation is going to get a lot worse for you."

There was venom in Regina's stare as she glared at Kate. "You going to arrest me because I got pissed about the law showing up at my house for no reason?" she spat. "Gonna arrest me because I told this nosy bitch what's what when she tried to listen to my conversation between me and your partner?"

"Ms. Voss, take three steps back," Kate said. "Do it now, and do it slowly."

Regina did as she was asked, but the steps she took were small and shuffling. And she somehow managed to stare daggers into all three of the other women all at once.

Kate then turned to the other woman. She still looked shaken but clearly relieved that someone had finally managed to calm Ms. Voss. "You, too," Kate said. "I need you to step back three steps."

The woman did, looking gratefully between Kate and DeMarco. Kate then turned back to Regina Voss and did her best to sound understanding rather than authoritative. "Ms. Voss, because this is your house, I'm going to allow you to tell me what happened. If you tell anything other than the truth, I'm going to have Agent DeMarco correct you. Sound good?"

There was still scorn on Regina's face, but she nodded. She brushed a few strands of her graying brown hair back and began. "Your partner came by my house, knocking on the door just as casual as you please. Asked me if she could ask some questions. I asked her what the questions were about and she wanted to know if I'd seen anything unusual in the neighborhood. And I said yes, I had. I told her there are far too many new people coming in this town, wasting space with these new houses and crowding up the all the real estate at the lake. It's always been bad, but it was terrible

this summer. I pointed out Mrs. Flair right there as an example."
She pointed to the woman in the running gear as she said this.
"She was walking down the street, right by my home, like she had
the right."

"Ms. Voss, she *does* have the right to walk down the street."

"Been there, tried that," DeMarco said.

"And then what happened, Ms. Voss?" Kate asked.

But Regina apparently had no interest in answering this. Kate
knew this was the part of the story where Regina Voss had been in
the wrong—where she had likely taken things too far. And since she
did not reply and the woman, Mrs. Flair, was clearly too scared to
talk, DeMarco filled in the rest.

"Mrs. Flair saw her pointing because we were standing right
there, inside the opened front door," DeMarco said. "Flair gave a
dismissive sort of wave to Ms. Voss and that was the end of it. Ms.
Voss came rushing out of the front door, damn near pushing me
over. She came out into the yard and started yelling. And that's
when you came up."

"Mrs. Flair, I take it from your attire you were out for a run?"
Kate said.

"Yes. I run three times a week. And for God's sake, I guess I
need to find a new route because this woman has had something
derogative to say about me each time I've come by here."

"You live around here?" Kate asked.

"A few blocks over," she said. "My husband and I moved into the
area a few months ago, just before summer."

"And had you ever met Ms. Voss before you started running by
here?"

"Not officially. Although when we were moving in, she was walking by our house and stood there, staring at us. Not bothering to
talk, not asking to help, nothing like that. Just giving us this mean,
glaring stare."

"Is that true?" Kate asked Regina Voss.

"Yes. And I am aware it was rude of me but... I'm done with
new families, new rich millennials and these spoiled grown-ups

able to retire at forty, coming into town and just taking it over." Her tone was nearing a scream again and Kate wasn't sure she had the patience for it. "Buying houses just to flip them and sell them to other people from out of town that come in and just try running the town."

"Mrs. Flair, please continue on your run," Kate said. "And yes…maybe find some alternate route in the future."

Flair nodded and carried on, though there was very little energy in her step when she started running again.

"You just let her go?" Regina asked. "Just like that?"

"She's done nothing wrong," DeMarco said.

"Not in your eyes. You know…none of these murders started happening until all of these new families started popping up. I looked into it a few days ago. Total murders in Estes over the past twenty-five years…one. A single murder. And that was an estranged wife, stabbing her husband. But then these new families come in…over the last three years, there have been multiple break-ins, noisy ass cars going up and down the road at all hours and now, over the past week, three murders. So yes…I'm a little pissed at the state of my hometown."

"Ms. Voss, that's understandable," Kate said. "But you can't take it out on everyone that passes by your house."

"And why not?"

"Because it's not *your* town," DeMarco said.

Kate cringed a bit at the sarcastic tone in DeMarco's voice. She had no doubt her partner had not don't it intentionally, but it was there.

"I may not own the town," Regina said. "But I own property in the town and have more of a stake in it than these assholes that come in to buy properties only to flip them and resell them. You don't know what it's like and quite frankly, I'd love it if you'd get the fuck out of my face!"

Regina then took one large stride toward DeMarco, getting in her face. She was screaming at the top of her lungs when she did, further going on and on about the state of Estes and how much she loathed the direction it was headed. Kate reached for her to pull her back but by then, it was a little too late.

Maybe it was the certain way she said a word or maybe it was intentional—but somehow, some of Regina Voss's spit ended up striking DeMarco right between the eyes.

"Thanks for that," DeMarco said.

Then, in a move so fast Kate was barely able to register it, DeMarco grabbed Regina by the left arm, spun her around with it, and brought up behind her back. She slapped a pair of cuffs on her and adjusted them up with both of Regina's hands bound behind her back. The entire series of movements took less than five seconds. To Kate, it was almost like watching a magic act.

Honestly, Kate thought it was a bit much, but said nothing. She reminded herself that she was here to support DeMarco. And besides, nothing she had just done would be sufficient to be reprimanded for. In Kate's eyes, it had just been a bit rough in terms of handling a semi-delusional woman in her fifties. What sort of woman in her right mind came charging at a federal agent like that?

"If you like the town of Estes so much," DeMarco said, "let's show you the police station."

"Oh, I'm familiar with it," Regina said through clenched teeth.

As Kate and DeMarco marched Regina up onto her porch to place a call to Armstrong, Kate thought: *I don't doubt that one bit.*

Sheriff Armstrong pulled up alongside the curb in her patrol car less than five minutes later. By that time, Kate and DeMarco had Regina Voss on her porch. Regina was standing with her back pressed against the side of the house so no passersby could see the cuffs. Kate was sitting in the little wicker chair Regina kept by the front door while DeMarco stood at the steps.

Armstrong looked like a woman who might be on the way to defuse a bomb rather than get caught up on the arrest.

"Ms. Voss, were you not hospitable to these ladies?" Armstrong asked.

At first, her approach irritated Kate. But then she thought that being the head of law enforcement of a town this small probably meant you got to know most of your town's residents very well. And if Regina Voss was someone who had indeed seen the inside of the police department before (as she had hinted at), then Armstrong likely knew how to talk to her without getting her riled up again.

"No, I wasn't," Regina said. "This younger one came asking me about anything I'd seen that might be out of the ordinary. I figured she was here to look into the murders and I wasn't sure if she was asking me as if I was a suspect or just an interested citizen."

"So why are you in cuffs?" Armstrong asked.

Regina made a prissy face and shrugged. She looked out to the road as if she were completely uninterested in what was going on. Or perhaps, Kate thought, almost daring Mrs. Flair to come jogging by again.

DeMarco took the liberty of filling Armstrong in. The sheriff nodded along, wincing here and there. When DeMarco's account of events was through, Armstrong waved the agents down into the yard. She looked back at Voss and asked: "You aren't going to be any trouble if I leave you right there for a few minutes, are you?"

"No. You go on out there and talk about me." She sneered when she said it, but there was also something in her expression that looked satisfied. Kate figured she was the type of crotchety middle-aged lady who liked it when people were talking about her—even if it was about negative things.

Armstrong led them to where she had parked her car and they gathered around the hood. "Regina Voss is a bitch," she said. "She has a sad story to justify it—two failed marriages, the latest of which saw her forty-nine-year-old husband leave town with a twenty-two-year-old tourist. That was three years ago and ever since then, she's been that local that all the kids make up stories about. Crazy old Ms. Voss, always yelling at anyone that dares to linger in front of her house for too long. Kids sometimes egg her house. She's *that* sort of woman. But she also loathes tourists and anyone new who comes into town. And the Flair family, as you might have picked up, are rather new. And between the three of us, Emily Flair bears a striking resemblance to the young lady who stole the second husband away."

"Regina hinted at the fact she'd been in trouble with law enforcement before," DeMarco said. "Anything serious?"

"A few verbal confrontations, one physical altercation that was nothing more than a slap that busted another woman's lip, and a vandalization charge."

"What did she vandalize?" Kate asked.

"Several real estate signs, out in front of new builds a few houses down. That was last year. She was caught in the act by one of my officers and she was quite proud of herself."

"I assume you don't think she's capable of murder?" DeMarco asked.

Armstrong nearly said something... her tongue and lips poised to say *No*. But then she stopped and considered it for a moment. "I'm inclined to say no," she said. "But with three people dead and no potential suspects, I wouldn't rule it out. She's mean-spirited, there's no doubt about that."

"I don't know," Kate said. "She looks pretty scrawny. And she has to be at least fifty-five. You think she could throw a woman five feet across open air from a second-floor landing? Or string someone up with a noose?"

"Like I said, I'm inclined to say no. But you know what? She's already cuffed. Might as well take her in and question her. Even if it's not her, I'm sure she's pissed off more than enough people. Maybe she could give us some names. She tries to stay up to date on new people that have moved into Estes."

DeMarco especially seemed to like this idea, taking the lead as the trio headed back up to the front porch. Armstrong willingly took the duty of letting Regina know that she would be taking a trip to the station, not primarily because of her behavior toward the agents but because they wanted to ask her some questions. Kate was expecting another outburst, but Regina remained calm. She did not look at all happy to be going, but it appeared as if the reality of what she had done was sinking in and she was accepting her punishment.

Still, she was quite glad when DeMarco elected to sit in the back of the car with her as they all piled into Armstrong's cruiser. Armstrong drove straight ahead, passing straight through the intersection Kate had been standing at less than twenty minutes ago. As they drove by it, Kate looked out the window to where she had accidentally scared the stranger.

She wasn't surprised to see that the black Taurus was no longer there.

What *did* surprise her, though, was the little shiver of alarm that passed through her when she realized it was gone.

CHAPTER FIFTEEN

"You have got to be joking, right?"

Regina Voss wore an expression that rested somewhere between genuine amusement and absolute rage. It was an eerie look, one that Kate wasn't certain she had ever seen before.

"Ms. Voss, we have to consider all options here," DeMarco said. "And quite frankly, you're easily the meanest person we've met since entering Estes. If the shoe fits, and all that."

"So you really think that I have the power to not only bludgeon these women with some heavy instrument, but to then somehow lug them through a house, up some stairs, and then shove them over a rail? I suppose I should be flattered that I look so fit, but I'm too busy being absolutely stunned at your sheer idiocy."

Regina was sitting at the same table Greg Seamster had occupied not too long ago. She was staring up at Kate and DeMarco as if trying to figure out which one she thought might be the dumber one. It had been decided that Armstrong would sit this one out, hoping that the removal of anyone familiar might make Regina more prone to being honest and transparent the angrier she got.

And so far, it seemed to be working.

"Well, would you care to answer the original questions I came knocking to ask?" DeMarco asked.

"I answered what I could before things got out of hand. No, I have not seen anything out of the ordinary—aside from all the houses going up for sale. But it's the same this time of year just about every year, now isn't it?"

"You gave very vague answers before you inexplicably went off on a passing woman, yes," DeMarco said. "But that was not—"

"I should sue the hell out of you! Out of the local pissant police department *and* the FBI! This is outrageous! I'll sue for wrongful arrest. I'll have both your jobs before this is over!"

"Or, you could just answer our questions like a respectable citizen," DeMarco said. "Three women are dead, Ms. Voss. And with your working knowledge of people coming in and out of town, you could potentially help us. We are not trying to pin anything on you. We legitimately just want you to answer some questions."

"And what if I don't?"

"Well, then you start to look very suspicious," DeMarco said.

Kate noticed then, as Regina was leaning partially over the table, that the woman was hunching over slightly. She thought she had noticed something similar when she had been railing off on Flair and DeMarco but had assumed it was just her body's response to the stress. But now, she wasn't too sure.

"Ms. Voss, are you on any medications?" she asked.

Regina looked at her with a baffled expression, as if she hadn't understood the question. "What's that got to do with anything?"

"Maybe nothing," Kate said. "But it would be helpful if you'd just answer the question."

"Just a muscle relaxant," she snipped. "Skelaxin."

"For your back?" Kate asked, feeling the slight chance of Regina Voss being any sort of promising suspect slipping even further away.

"Yes. I have a herniated disc. Been bothering me for almost a year now and just won't get better. How'd you know that?"

"It's the way you're sitting."

Kate also thought: *Maybe it would get better if you could somehow curb that bad habit of rushing out onto your lawn to yell and scream at people.*

DeMarco turned to her and Kate could tell that the same thoughts were going through her mind. Voss was not a suspect. Kate doubted the woman could lift as much as twenty-five pounds.

And from what she had seen, the woman was not stealthy enough to sneak up on anyone, especially not in an empty house.

And honestly, if she was being this difficult, maybe it would be a blessing to just let her go back home and stew in her hatred in her home. Kate at least would be glad to be rid of her.

"One second, please, Ms. Voss," Kate said.

She and DeMarco exited the room. Kate was surprised to see a twitching smile on DeMarco's face. "How in the hell did we even begin to *think* she would be a suspect?"

"I think the attitude and sheer hatefulness is what did it for me," Kate said. "But even though we know she can't be a suspect, we're right to assume she would be a good source of neighborhood information."

"Yeah, the angry and nosy bitches always are," DeMarco said. She then sighed, shook her head, and added, "I'm sorry. That's not very professional of me."

"It's not. But it's true. Don't sweat it."

Armstrong, having seen them come out of the room, joined them about halfway down the hallway. She peered toward the interrogation room with her rms folded. "Nothing?" she asked.

"Nothing but a medical condition," Kate said. "Did you know she had a herniated disc in her back?"

"I did not. Want to me find out what doctor diagnosed it just to make sure she's on the up and up?"

"Might as well just to knock it off the list," DeMarco said. "But if she's the killer, I'll swim all the way across Fallows Lake buck naked."

"There's a strange mental picture," Kate said.

As Armstrong headed back toward the front of the building, Kate and DeMarco started back to the interrogation room. Just before they got there, Kate's phone rang. She paused before answering it because every call so far had come to DeMarco. As she reached for her phone, she wondered if it might be Allen.

She felt rather awkward when she saw that it was Director Duran. She thought of turning away and hiding it from DeMarco but she knew that would be childish. Instead, she went ahead and showed DeMarco the caller display. With a shrug (and a look of disappointment from DeMarco), Kate answered the call.

"I'm afraid you have the wrong agent," she said, trying to sound jovial. "This isn't my case."

"I appreciate the attempt at passive humor," Duran said, "but I frankly find nothing about this funny. Three bodies now, Wise. I thought you'd be able to draw this thing to a close."

"We're certainly working towards that goal, sir."

"And which of you suggested to the local real estate companies that a hold be placed on all showings for the time being?"

"I believe that was DeMarco, sir. But I agree with her one hundred percent."

It then occurred to her that the only way Duran would have known about this was if one of the real estate companies had contacted Armstrong or even the FBI directly. Apparently, not everyone thought it was the best idea. She understood it on a professional level, but she also hated that she and DeMarco were being second-guessed. To be twenty-six years old and feel as if someone were tattling on you was not a great feeling.

"Wise, you understand how much fear that causes, right? From what I understand, there are agents that are afraid to go just about anywhere now because of this."

"Maybe they should for now," she said. "Look, if someone has spoken to you about that decision, then I assume you also know it's a slow time for sales in the market. These homes have all been hard sales because now that the weather is turning cooler, no one really cares about looking for homes by the lake. All of these things were strongly considered before we made such a decision. And the only reason anyone cares now is because, aside from the dead agents, there is a fear that the murders will make the homes harder to sell."

"Well, I also know that the governor isn't happy. I had the displeasure of speaking to him as well. Kate, this is one of those cases that has the potential to turn very ugly and very public—very quickly. Do you understand?"

She had assumed this much but was really hoping it would not come to that. The fact that the last murder had occurred in a home the governor owned and was currently trying to sell made this case a hell of a lot more slippery.

"Let's get this thing wrapped. I'd really rather not have an entire team out there by the lake with the governor of the state of Delaware watching it all unfold."

They ended the call, Kate a little taken aback by Duran's demeanor. He was typically a down to earth man and was only ever disagreeable when he felt something was getting away from him. It made her wonder if he had been expecting more out of DeMarco and was regretting his decision to send her alone in the first place. Kate wondered if this had been an exploratory sort of case where he was trying to feel DeMarco out—maybe to see what sort of agent she'd be able to lead once Kate retired for good and DeMarco need to be paired up with someone else.

"How much of that did you hear?" Kate asked DeMarco.

"Enough."

"I don't know why he called me. Sorry, DeMarco."

"I do. There are three bodies now and I'm a young agent without a lot of experience. It's okay, Kate. You're the smarter choice here. I'm a big girl and I know that. It's okay."

"Still…" Kate said, feeling like she had unintentionally pulled the rug out from under her partner.

"So what do we do now?" DeMarco asked.

"We need to light some fires to get those lists from the real estate agencies," Kate said. "If we can get a complete list of every single person who had access to those houses, there has to be something there."

"We've struck out with it so far," DeMarco commented.

"So then we need to dig harder," Kate said, pulling out her phone to make a call to all three of the real estate agencies in the area.

DeMarco headed back into the interrogation room with Regina Voss while Kate started making her calls. She felt as if the case had shifted in the course of the past two minutes or so, that Duran's decision to call her rather than DeMarco had meant more than it seemed. It made her feel slightly guilty, but she could not let that get in the way of cracking this case. They could not assume that because all real estate showings were being placed on hold that the killer would stop.

It then occurred to her that perhaps the killer was only targeting real estate agents because they were easy prey. They typically ventured into nice homes by themselves in preparation for stagings or to take notes and pictures. Maybe now that they had made it much harder for him to target real estate agents, he'd move on to something else.

It felt like a flimsy theory, though. There had been three so far. It spoke of a connection, of some kind of grudge almost.

No, someone so committed would not be deterred because they had made it harder for him. Hell, someone like that might not even be aware that he was being investigated. To someone so committed, there might only be the murders in his life and nothing else. She'd seen it happen before and while some tended to think such a criminal would be easier to mind, it actually made them a little more elusive; they did not stick to ritual or schedule and were much less predictable.

If anything, it might get him thinking more creatively. And that could be the worst thing possible for the case.

CHAPTER SIXTEEN

He'd nearly had a panic attack when the woman had coming knocking at his driver's side window. At first he'd just assumed she was nothing more than some nosy bitch, unable to stand seeing someone parked in front of a house and not knowing why. But within just a few moments, he had gotten the feeling that she had been there on purpose. She'd had the look of a woman who was looking for something.

He had watched her walk quickly away from his car, drawn away by something else. When she was around the corner and out of sight, he'd looked to his piece of lumber almost lovingly before starting the engine to his Taurus and pulling to the end of the street. When he spotted the woman speaking to two other women in a rather heated way, he turned left and drove away from them. He checked the rearview a few times as he made his escape and as far as he could tell, he was never followed.

With no clear place left to go, he drove around Estes for a while. He headed out toward the lake, driving slowly along the stretch of highway that etched itself along the water for about a mile and a half. It was oddly calming—which was exactly what he needed. He knew that some people preferred the ocean to the lake, but the lake had always calmed him. The lake was still and contained, whereas the ocean was endless and raging, its depths unknown.

He was well aware that his work was going to be much harder now. The police had been swarming for the past few days and while the Estes police force wasn't very big and, in his opinion, not to be taken too seriously, he knew he could not underestimate them.

After all, even a hornet's nest looked mostly non-threatening if you were standing far enough away from it. But when it was stirred, things could get quite dangerous.

It made him wonder if the woman who had bothered him earlier was some sort of law enforcement. Maybe she was a detective, or someone sent in from the State Police to help the Estes force. The conversation she'd started with him certainly made her seem as if she had some sort of agenda. If she *had* been some sort of cop or detective or something like that, she had nearly had him. Had she not been distracted by something else, it might all be over for him right now.

The very idea made him nervous. It made him want to go ahead with his original plans, not worried that he might get caught. But really... of course he did not want to get caught. He just needed to calm down, needed to think. He had known from the start that it would get harder with each death. But he had not expected it to get so difficult so *fast*.

He couldn't let this little setback discourage him, though. After all, so far he was in the clear. No one suspected a thing. He was reminded of just how well he had done as he stopped by a gas station and pumped a tank of gas. Someone he vaguely knew waved at him as they passed by. Not once did anyone look at him as if they suspected anything. No one knew what he was up to. No one knew how he was getting into the houses, sleeping there and studying the schedules of the agents and builders.

This sense of freedom and power gave him the nerve he needed to start working toward his next step. He left the road that ran along the side of Fallows Lake and headed deeper into Estes, where the lakeside community gave way to what started to look more like a typical well-to-do neighborhood. Taking a chance, he drove back by the home he had been parked in front of an hour ago when the woman had tapped on his window. The woman was no longer there, and the trio was no longer standing on the sidewalk. That made him feel much better, too.

Relieved, he headed back into familiar territory. He could have probably taken the route blindfolded. Within another ten minutes, he was pulling his car into the parking lot of Davis and Hopper Realty. The lot was L-shaped, the front portion used by the agents and clients, the side portion used by customers of the liquor store and marketing company that rented out space on the back half of the lot.

He parked on the side space, beside the green pickup truck. He'd been here enough to know that the green truck belonged to one of the owners of the marketing company. The truck always parked in the same space. By parking beside the truck, he could still see almost the entire lot over at Davis and Hooper. And because it was a fairly quiet part of town (hell, weren't they *all* quiet areas in a town like Estes?), he had no fear of being seen. Even if he *was* seen, no one would think much of it. He was not memorable, though some people in Estes knew his face. He'd never been a memorable type. And while it was something he had felt sad about in his youth, it was paying off now.

The woman in charge of showing the house he had been parked in front of earlier in the day was named Monique Whorley. He'd been following her for just as long as he'd been following the other three, but she tended to show fewer properties. The ones she *did* show, though, were usually high-end homes. Of course, nothing really moved this time of year in Estes, so that meant she wasn't getting out of the office much.

He'd been camped in front of her latest home earlier, fairly certain she was due to go by. When she had not shown up, he'd started to wonder if the agencies were starting to make adjustments, perhaps frightened by the likelihood of a murderer that seemed to be targeting agents. When the strange woman had knocked on his window, it had strengthened that suspicion. And now, the fact that Monique had still not made it out to the house made it a damn near certainty.

He sat there for another thirty-five minutes, eyeing the adjacent side of the parking lot. He sat bolt upright in his seat when Monique came out. She walked slowly across the lot, a slightly overweight African American woman with a bright smile. But she was not smiling today. In fact, she looked rather somber. Probably sad about the recent deaths. All of the agents knew one another. In fact, he knew that two or three of them were sleeping together, in some weird little love triangle. He'd heard two agents chatting about it last week while he'd been rooted down in the crawlspace of a house out closer to the lake.

He watched as Monique unlocked her car and opened the driver's side door. He smiled as he watched her, wondering if it was really going to be this easy. He gripped the steering wheel in anticipation, feeling that familiar excitement sweep through him. If she was going to the house he had been perched in front of earlier, that would be it. He'd kill her and move on to—

A man came out of the Davis and Hooper building, hurrying to catch up with her. The two of them had a brief conversation over the hood of her car as he approached the passenger's side door. He opened the door, got in, and the car slowly pulled away.

From his seat in his Taurus, he watched the car pull off. Disappointment and sharp anger overcame him. He hissed numerous curses under his breath, the words coming out with such force between his clenched teeth that spit came out, spattering the windshield. He felt himself starting to lose control but shut it down instantly. He pushed it all down; it felt like swallowing hot tar.

He could either lose his shit or he could follow her. So what if someone else was with her? So what if the recent swarm of police activity was going to make his work more difficult?

He thought of his mother and what she would think of her son, the quitter. Her son, the moron who shut down at the least hint of change and threw a hissy fit.

"To hell with it," he said.

He cranked the car, peeled out of the parking spot, and followed after Monique Whorley and her passenger.

CHAPTER SEVENTEEN

The complete set of lists came quickly, as the very real threat of having to shut down all real estate transactions for an unknown amount of time suddenly had all three agencies far beyond cooperative. With Regina Voss released and sent back home (still shouting threats of suing everyone under God's bright yellow sun), Kate and DeMarco were left alone once again, scouring the lists and making calls while Armstrong worked with her small force to interview the local families and friends of the deceased agents.

"I suppose this could be much worse," DeMarco said as she looked over the list that had been sent in by Crest Realty. "Can you imagine the length of this kind of a list in DC? Or New York?"

Kate made a whistling noise, not even wanting to imagine that kind of horror. It made her very grateful for the comparatively short list she now held in her hands. It was the list from Lakeside Realty and was only thirteen people deep. Actually, it should have been twenty or so people deep, but the names of several of the Sheetrock contractors could not be found; Kate wasn't too surprised, as she knew it was nothing unusual to have undocumented workers on the manual labor front.

She crossed through the names they had already spoken to, and the fact that it left only eight names left her feeling hopeless. She knew that if there were no leads on this list, the case was going to be incredibly difficult and certainly be unable to solve on the quickened timeline Duran had given them.

"DeMarco, can I see that list from Crest?" she asked.

DeMarco slid it across the table to her. Kate saw that DeMarco had also already crossed through a few names on her own list. Hers was narrowed down to only five names, making it that much easier for Kate to see two names that were also on the Lakeside list. With a sudden childlike excitement, Kate drew an asterisk by each one.

"Two similarities on these two lists," Kate said. She turned the papers around so that DeMarco could see them.

"You know, the name Roger Carr was on the very short list we got from Davis and Hopper, too." DeMarco dug around in the several piles of paper they had accumulated, found the list, and checked it. "Yeah, right here. Roger Carr, the appraiser on most of the homes Crest Realty has sold in the last five years."

"But this other name similar on Lakeside and Crest—Margie Phelps—she's not on the Davis and Hopper list."

"Correct. Phelps does staging, I believe. Still, two out of three seems legit to me," DeMarco said.

"So, let's go pay them both a visit," Kate said. "At the very least, they might be able to give us some information about squatters. I'm starting to understand it might be a larger problem than I'd originally thought."

Though she never felt truly effective when tracking down a lead that had been culled from a list, Kate managed to feel upbeat as she and DeMarco left the station and headed back out into Estes. While it might be a bit premature to get excited over one similarity between two of the Realtors, having *two* was too promising to ignore.

Roger Carr's home was located less than ten minutes away from the police station. He lived in a small row of townhouses that, while not decrepit by any means, were easily on the lower end of residences in Estes. It seemed strange to Kate, as she figured an appraiser for homes in an area around a lake would be quite wealthy.

They knocked on his door and got no answer. After they knocked a second time, they stepped away as DeMarco used her phone to search for his business name and number. She called the number listed under Carr Appraisals and Estimates and placed the call on speakerphone as she and Kate got back into the car.

The call was answered by an older-sounding lady with a pleasant grandmotherly voice.

"I need to speak with Roger Carr, please," DeMarco said.

"I'm sorry, but he's out on a job right now," the lady said. "He's due back in a few hours, though, if you'd like to leave a message."

"No thank you," DeMarco said. "But I do need to speak with him quite urgently about a property in the area. Would you happen to know the address he is currently visiting?"

Kate grinned. It was smart of DeMarco not to pull the FBI card just yet. An older lady in a small community likely had a sense of loyalty to her employer, and there was no telling how she might respond to having the FBI call, looking for her boss.

"Oh, I see! Well, hold on one second...the address is right here...ah, here we are. He's out at 422 Hammermill. You know where it is?"

"Yes ma'am," DeMarco said as Kate instantly started the engine. "Thanks so much."

DeMarco ended the call and they shared a look that was almost the equivalent of exchanging a telepathic thought. In the end, it was Kate who spoke it out loud as she backed out of the lot.

"Hammermill is the same street Tamara Bateman was killed on."

With it spoken out loud, the entire scenario felt more urgent. While there was no smoking gun just yet, Kate couldn't help but feel that they were at least headed in the right direction.

To get to 422 Hammermill, they had to drive by the house Bea Faraday had been killed in. Kate was not superstitious by any means, but she couldn't help but feel as if this was some sort of an omen. When they pulled up in front of the property at 422, it occurred to Kate for the first time that a community like this one must always be in a certain state of flux: vacationers coming and going, people with a midlife crisis on their hands, buying and then promptly selling lakeside properties, the unpredictability of the summer season. It had to be a slight nightmare for real estate companies and land developers.

And a surefire annoyance to residents like Regina Voss.

The house was a basic two-story with no clear style. The few cracks along the sidewalk indicated that it was not a new build, though the yard looked to have been recently mowed and it was clear to even Kate's untrained eye that the siding had been power washed. They walked up to the front door with a sense of urgency. Kate wasn't quite convinced that the killer might be inside, but she did feel that the coincidence of it all was far too much to be ignored.

Kate knocked on the door, waited just a second, and then opened it. When she and DeMarco stepped inside, they entered a formal-looking living room. There was no furniture and the carpet had recently been cleaned, the acrid scent of carpet shampoo clinging to the air. In front of them, a split dining and kitchen area sat to the right and directly ahead, while a wide hallway branched off to the left.

There were two people in the kitchen, both male. One was standing, leaning slightly against the kitchen counters, while the other stood by the large dining room window. They both regarded Kate and DeMarco with bemused expressions, though the man standing in the kitchen also looked rather annoyed.

"Um ... can we help you, ladies?" he asked.

"Yes," DeMarco said. "Is one of you Roger Carr?"

"That's me," the man in the kitchen said. "Can I ask who you might be, and how you knew I was here?"

"We'd like to speak with you privately," DeMarco said, quickly cutting her eyes in the direction of the other man.

"No thank you," Carr said. "Here is fine."

"If you say so," DeMarco said. She then pulled out her badge and ID, showing it to both of the men with staged enthusiasm.

"Mr. Carr, we're with the FBI and need to speak to you regarding a string of recent murders in the area."

Carr was so shocked that he took a step back. He looked to the other man as if hoping he might have something to say. But the man was clearly speechless. As the man turned more proportionately toward Kate and DeMarco, Kate saw that there was a Crest Realty log embroidered on the chest of his shirt.

"Think we could speak privately now?" Kate asked with a little grin.

The Crest employee instantly started walking in their direction, his eyes locked on the door.

"Before you go," Kate said, "do you mind telling us why you're here?"

"I was meeting with Mr. Carr to get notes on his appraisal of the place. We're looking for anything we can to knock the price down a bit more."

The Crest employee was on the young side, maybe thirty or just a little north of it, but he looked like a cornered little child as he answered. Kate almost felt sorry for him.

"Thank you," DeMarco said.

"Hey, Pete," Roger Carr called from the kitchen. "Maybe keep this to yourself for now."

Pete, the Crest agent, only nodded as he made his way to the door and made a swift exit. With him gone, the agent both looked back to Carr. He was slowly moving out of the kitchen, doing anything he could to not be cornered by them.

"You came into a property I was appraising for work," Carr said, as if trying to work it all out for himself. "I take that to mean you either think I know something or that I did it. That about right?"

"We're hoping your answers to some questions might help to clear that all up," DeMarco said.

Carr seemed understandably hesitant. He appeared to be in his early fifties, his brown hair and beard having started to show a touch of gray. Kate wasn't sure why, but she thought he looked somewhat disgruntled. It was in his eyes, the way he glanced back and forth between them. She thought he assumed they had already made up their minds about him. He had a shifty look about him, the kind of man who was likely used to talking his way out of anything.

"I'll answer what I can," he said.

"First," DeMarco said, "I should tell you that our reason for coming to you is because out of the three lists we have for people who had access to the three homes in which real estate agents were recently killed, your name was the only one that appeared on all three of them."

"That's really not all that surprising," Carr said. "I'm currently the only appraiser around here. It's been that way for the last eight months or so. There was one other guy, but he packed up and headed out to the beach. As you can imagine, that keeps me pretty busy."

"The guy that just left said you two were looking for ways to bring the price on this home down," DeMarco said. "Isn't part of your job to make sure the seller gets the most they can for the home?"

Carr gave a stealthy smile at this comment, but nodded. "Usually, yes. And I guarantee you that's exactly what my former competitor is doing these days. Jacking up those beachfront prices. But here at the lake, things are different."

"You seemed to already know about the three murders," Kate said. "How did you find out about them?"

"I actually only knew about Tamara Bateman first. Didn't hear about Bea Faraday or Dhayna Tsui until late last night, when I was informed that we were likely looking at a hold on all real estate transactions until a killer is found."

"Did you know any of the agents who were murdered?" Kate asked.

"I'd seen all of them here and there over the last year or so. A smaller community like this one, it's unavoidable. But I'd say I worked with Bea more than anyone else."

"Could you tell us why you were looking for reasons to sell this home for *less*?" DeMarco asked.

That stealthy smile came back as he answered. It made Kate not fully trust him.

"Because there are so many homes that are just sitting stagnant on the market around here. We can drop prices without anyone asking why, but most buyers feel more comfortable if they *know* why. It especially helps if we can find reasons that most people would find superficial."

He was all but chuckling as he said this. It made Kate wonder what other slightly dishonest practices he might revel in.

"Do you find something amusing about it?" she asked.

"That's not quite the right word. But seeing as how my own contracting business sort of went under during the last housing crisis, seeing these overpriced homes coming down in price so rapidly *does* bring a bit of a smile to my face."

"How badly will the murders affect the sale of homes in the area?" Kate asked.

"Well, it's going to essentially destroy any chance of the homes the agents were killed in," Carr said. "Those will have to go way under asking price and it'll take a few weeks, if not months, for them to sell. As for other properties in the area, it might spook *some* buyers. But buyers from out of town likely won't care. But we'll probably have to sell surrounding properties for just as cheap as the affected properties just to even things out—for a while."

"You've seen it before, I take it?" Kate asked.

"Actually, no. But once you get closer to the beach, this thing becomes a little more common. There are even houses where former owners had been busted for selling drugs out of the home that are tough sells."

"What about the house we're in right now?" DeMarco. "The home Tamara Bateman was killed in is just a block up the street."

"It'll probably come down about eight grand in price. When that drop doesn't move it, it'll likely come to a final asking price somewhere around twenty grand south of where it would have originally been listed."

"Mr. Carr, in your line of work, have you ever had an issue with squatters?"

He did chuckle this time. "No, not squatters. I did come across a teenage couple doing things their folks likely wouldn't have approved of. It was a house that had been on the market for a while, so I guess they just assumed it was abandoned and free for grabs—no pun intended."

Even the way Carr said *no pun intended* rubbed Kate the wrong way. It was rare that she came across someone she simply didn't like upon appearances, but Roger Carr was one of those people. She thought about the condition of his home, despite the fact that he was obviously a very busy man with a fairly lucrative job. Of course, he had mentioned his previous company going under not too long ago during the housing crisis. She wondered if there had been bankruptcy involved. Maybe he had lost everything, placing him in one of those very modest townhouses.

And maybe that's why he's borderline gleeful about all of these homes having to come down in price, she thought. *Maybe he sees it as some sort of justice. And maybe, if he's just deranged enough, his previous woes could be motive to kill real estate agents. A stretch, sure… but there's just something about him that feels off.*

"Do you mind telling us exactly why your company went out of business?" Kate asked.

"Same as any other business," he said. His tone indicated that he thought it was an incredibly stupid question. "Money. As in, I wasn't bringing enough of it in. When people realize they can't afford new homes, there's not much work for a contractor. Especially not in an area like this. As you can see, though, I managed to keep a job in the industry. I like the appraisal end much better. There's much less stress and commitment. The money isn't quite as good, but it's not bad."

DeMarco reached out and handed Carr one of her business cards. "Mr. Carr, whether you like it or not, your presence at all three houses so far makes you the only person we know that could potentially answer questions about the properties and the agents themselves. We'd appreciate it if you'd try to remain available for the next few days."

Carr looked at the business card and gave a curt little nod. When he placed the card into his pocket, he looked as if it was a huge inconvenience to him. "Yeah, I'll be around. But as I've said…I'm very busy."

"Might not be if anyone else around here dies, though," Kate said. It was an unnecessary and slightly immature jab, but she didn't care.

Carr had nothing to say to that. The three of them stood there awkwardly until DeMarco started walking back toward the front door. Kate followed her, leaving Carr to his business inside.

"Initial thoughts?" DeMarco asked.

"Honestly? I think he's a creep, but I couldn't tell you why."

"Same here. But I don't feel like he fits the profile of our killer."

"Why's that?" Kate asked. She felt he had slight motivations but she, too, thought it unlikely that he was the killer.

"Hard to say. I think he just seems like the sort of guy that has to always be in control. But in an anal-retentive sort of way. I think murder has too many question marks, too many different ways things could go wrong. So I don't think he'd be able to make himself do it—if he was even that sort of man in the first place."

Kate was impressed. It was a very rational way to think, and, now that she thought of it, pretty on the nose. It was actually a much clearer picture of why she had not cared for him at first glance.

"Let's give the staging woman a call," DeMarco said as they got back into the car. "Maybe she'll be a bit warmer than Mr. Carr."

They pulled away from the vacant house, Kate pulling up the address for Margie Phelps's place of business. Along the way, Kate eyed each house with a FOR SALE sign in its yard, wondering if the killer had been viewing that house recently as well. It made her think of the man she had spied in the black Taurus just before she's had the misfortune of being introduced to Regina Voss. Something about that brief encounter did not sit well with her.

They were running out of time. With the governor involved, Duran would now be watching this case very closely. She feared if they didn't have at least a promising lead within a handful of hours, the little town of Estes was going to be overrun with State Police and federal agents. And all that would do, as far as Kate was concerned, was edge her and DeMarco out.

And at fifty-six years old, she never knew which case could be her last. And if it was this one, she'd be damned if she would be pushed out of it.

CHAPTER EIGHTEEN

Simple Touch Staging might have been one of the cutest businesses Kate had ever stepped foot in. It was located right in the heart of Estes, about a block away from all of the waterfront properties along the lake. The building was small, tucked in between an Italian restaurant and a gift shop, but was warm and inviting. The entire building consisted of one room, split up by two decorative wall dividers. When Kate and DeMarco entered, there were two women at a small workstation in the front of the building. One was sitting at a computer monitor, the other standing behind her.

They both looked in the direction of the agents as they entered. The woman standing greeted them with a smile while the second woman remained focused on the computer monitor.

"How can I help you?" the standing woman asked. She was tall and slender with red hair. She looked to be in her forties, though the excessive makeup she wore made it very hard to tell.

"We were hoping to speak with Margie Phelps," Kate said.

The tall woman turned to the other woman at the computer. She was now looking at them again, apparently shocked to have heard her name called. "That's me," she said. "What can I do for you?"

It was clear that she did not want to leave whatever she was working on, but she came to the little counter area at the front of the building, joining her tall co-worker as dutifully as she could manage.

The taller woman gave a polite nod and, seeing that she was not needed, went back over to the workstation and picked up where Margie Phelps had left off.

"Ms. Phelps," Kate said, "we're with the FBI. Agents Wise and DeMarco. We wanted to talk to you about the three recent murders in the area. We know that you had recently been contracted to work on two of the homes, correct?"

"That's right. The one on Leander and the one on Hammermill. God...these murders. I knew Dhayna fairly well. I can't believe what's happened."

"How well did you know her?" DeMarco asked.

"Well about seven or eight years ago, she and I met up with a group of friends every Tuesday night for margaritas down at Jake's on the Lake. But then we grew up, I guess. We still knew one another, but it was just quick hellos on the street, you know? I hadn't had a real conversation with her in nearly a year or so, I guess."

"Any idea if she had a boyfriend or estranged family in the area?"

"I don't know about a boyfriend, but I know she has no family around here. I believe her mother died when Dhayna was quite young. And her father lives somewhere out west. Arizona or New Mexico or something like that."

"What about the other victims?" DeMarco asked. "Did you know them?"

"I knew *of* them. I mean, I knew who they were, but never really knew them well. We've staged homes for all three of the real estate companies in the area so we all sort of weave in and out of each other's work lives, you know?"

"Can you think of anyone in the local scene who might have a grudge against the real estate companies?"

Margie thought about it for a moment before shaking her head. "None that I can think of."

"How about past agents?" Kate asked. "I ask you because, as you might imagine, the real estate companies aren't very likely to give up the names of former employees as potential leads in a triple-murder investigation."

Rather than answer, Margie turned and looked to the woman sitting at the computer monitor. She was no longer paying attention to whatever was on the screen, but had instead started listening in to their conversation.

"Janell, you want to take that one?"

The taller woman, Janell, sighed and gave a shrug. "I don't know if the timing of it would even work out," she said. "And really, I hate to even make such an assumption."

"What assumption?" Kate asked.

"There's a moving company that we work with pretty closely," Margie said. "We'll stage the home and the movers will sometimes use our plans to set up the furniture and things like that."

"If I'm being honest, the only guy in the whole company I trust is the owner," Janell said. "He's a good guy... an older gentleman. But some of the men he has working for him are pretty gross. Always whistling at us and cat-calling. Things like that. There was one day last week when I was out at a property by the lake that they were taking furniture into. I was in the kitchen, playing around with different place settings, while they were setting up the den. One of the hired guys just sort of lost it. Yelling at the owner about money and time off. I thought it was going to turn into a fight. This guy, he pushed James, the boss, pretty hard and then left."

"And you saw this all go down?" Kate asked.

"Yeah, I was standing right there in the kitchen when it happened. He threw a lamp across the den and I think he even kicked a headlight out of the moving truck that was parked in the driveway. Started screaming about how he was going to beat the crap out of his boss and his coworkers. It was pretty scary. "

"You know anything about this guy?"

"Just his first name," Janell said. "And that's because some of the other guys said his name a few times as they were trying to get him to calm down: Matt. I don't know a last name."

"And what's the name of that moving company?"

"Mulligan Movers," Margie said. "Owned by a guy named Jack Mulligan."

This time, it was Kate who offered a business card, sliding it across the little counter toward the women. "Please let us know if you think of anything else, or hear anything from your clients."

"Of course," Margie said.

They left the little business with Kate comfortable ruling out Margie Phelps of any sort of foul play. And while she knew a disgruntled employee from a moving company might not exactly be a promising lead, at least it was something. She was also starting to understand that in a small town like Estes, Delaware, the real estate community was rather tight-knit. So maybe a disgruntled employee with some grievances to air might be just the sort of lead they were looking for.

Chapter Nineteen

"I'm looking for Jack Mulligan, please."

"That's me," the man on the other end of the line said. Kate thought he had the kind of voice that would make for a great story-telling grandfather someday.

"Mr. Mulligan, my name is Kate Wise. I'm a special agent with the FBI. I was hoping you might have some time to talk about a former employee named Matt. I understand that he recently quit in a dramatic fashion."

"Well, yeah, he did. But with all due respect, I'm not too sure looking into that employee would be worth your time."

"Why is that?"

There was a dry chuckle from Jack Mulligan's throat. "Matt was a good worker for sure, but he's got one hell of a temper on him. You mind me asking why you want to talk with him?"

"Sorry, sir. I can't really say at this point."

"Well, you're welcome to ask what you want but I honestly think Matt is all bark and no bite. Nowadays anyway. I know he had a rocky past and all but... I think he might be a good soul down deep."

Kate appreciated Jack's attempt at protecting a former employee. But she also knew that many profiles of people who committed homicide sounded just like that. Especially when the suspect already had a history—recently going so far as to threaten violence on the people he worked with.

"I appreciate the sentiment," Kate said, "but all the same, time is of the essence, and I was hoping you might be able to tell me the best way to get in touch with him."

Jack was quiet for a moment, perhaps trying to decide if he truly wanted to give the information. Finally, he sighed and answered: "I can give you his phone number and address," he said. "But let me warn you … if his wife is there, you may want to keep your distance. I spoke with her this morning. She asked if I could send her his last check. This was the third job he's quit in a year and she's plenty pissed."

"Thanks, but we'll take our chances."

After Jack gave her the information, she thanked him and plugged the address into the map application on her phone. Being that Estes wasn't a large town at all, Kate wasn't surprised to see that the address was less than ten miles away.

"Full name is Matt Redman," Kate told DeMarco. "Twenty-nine years old and, according to Jack Mulligan, built like a slab of granite."

"Much more promising than a middle-aged woman with a bad back," DeMarco commented.

They both chuckled at this as they headed directly along the edge of the lake, the afternoon sunlight sparkling from the water beside them.

Matt Redman lived in a small apartment complex located about a mile away from the nearest lake access. The apartment complex was similar to the townhouses they had visited while looking for Roger Carr. The building was two stories tall, connected by stairways built into concave entryways.

Redman's place was on the second floor. They passed by two men standing outside, one vaping while the other griped about politics. The blasting of rap music could be heard from a few doors down, but it wasn't outrageous. The place seemed mostly quiet, like the rest of the town as it mourned the loss of summer crowds and income.

They came to his apartment, and DeMarco knocked on the door. Kate was happy to let her assume the lead here; after the phone call from Duran earlier, Kate wanted to give DeMarco every opportunity she could to regain some of her confidence.

Immediately after DeMarco knocked, they could hear heavy footfalls coming toward the door. They were moving fast, as if the person inside was expecting company. When the door opened, it was not Matt Redman they saw, but a very angry-looking woman. She was slightly overweight and wearing a very thin T-shirt with no bra, and gym shorts. When the woman spotted two women at the door, her face scrunched up into a comical-looking confusion.

"Who the hell are you?" the woman asked.

DeMarco had no qualms about showing her badge and ID in response to the rude question. "Agents DeMarco and Wise, FBI. We're looking for Matt Redman."

"That makes three of us," the woman said. "He's not here. Hasn't been since about ten o'clock this morning when he told me he quit his job. Asshole had been hiding it from me for a few days."

"Do you know what he has been doing these last few days, if not going to work?"

"I don't know. My guess is hanging out at one of the bars around town. He's no prize, so I don't think I need to worry that he's been having an affair."

"Mrs. Redman, can you—"

"What the hell does the FBI want him for? What's he been doing?" She looked slightly alarmed, but anger appeared to still be her first expression.

"His name came up in the investigation into three recent murders."

The anger faded, though just for a moment. Mrs. Redman's face went slack, as she was clearly shocked. She uttered: "Shit."

"We just need to speak with him," Kate cleared up. "He's not a suspect."

This wasn't entirely true; they had no way of knowing what sort of man they might be dealing with. But still, she knew that an angry spouse was usually going to be a reliable source of information As screwed up as it seemed, Kate was sure that if they kept her angry, she might reveal something that could help them.

"Do you have any idea where he might be?" DeMarco asked.

A thin smile came over Mrs. Redman's lips. Kate supposed she was relishing the fact that she was about to send the FBI on her husband's tail.

"I know exactly where he is. He went down to his favorite bar—Jake's on the Lake. When you two came knocking, I thought it was him."

"Thank you, Mrs. Redman."

"You feel free to let him know I was the one that told you where he was. And then tell him if he wants a wife anymore, he better bring his sorry ass back home."

Neither agent said anything to this. Even if she'd wanted to say something, Kate had no idea how to respond to something like that. They turned away, and Kate heard the woman closing the door rather roughly behind them.

"Well, I think it's clear she isn't so sure her husband would be capable of murder," DeMarco said.

"But she wouldn't mind getting him into trouble … making him sweat a bit, anyway."

"So let's go make him sweat," DeMarco said.

Jake's on the Lake was a strange establishment, as it seemed to cater to two different lifestyles all at once. On the far end, a long pier extended out onto the lake. The bar area, located under a beautifully decorated awning, looked rather high scale. Kate assumed this had been the part of Jake's at the Lake that Margie Phelps and her friends had once met for drinks. The other half of the place was tucked away inside. There was a second bar located to the right and just behind the central dining area. It was dimly lit and had the eerie glow of most smaller bars, illuminated by generic neon signs advertising light beer and TV screens perched behind it.

It was 2:28 in the afternoon on a Thursday, and the bar was relatively dead. Three people sat at the bar—a younger couple on one end, sipping from dark beers, and a lone man sitting in the center. His back was hunched and he sat in a slouched position, as if protecting whatever he was drinking.

They approached the lone man, DeMarco giving Kate the nod to go first. Kate did, approaching the bar and the lone man. "Mind if I sit here?" she asked.

The man looked up at her, narrowed his eyes, and shrugged. "Plenty of other stools here, but sure. You can sit here if you want."

Kate didn't think he was drunk yet, but he was rapidly approaching it. There was no skepticism in his voice or glare, just annoyance. She wondered if he might have offered more attention if DeMarco had taken the stool instead. She was well aware that at fifty-six, she was not quite the visual bait she had once been.

"Are you Matt Redman, by any chance?" she asked.

The man turned back to her right away. She had his attention now, the irritation in his eyes now replaced by confusion and anger.

"My wife send you?" he asked. When he said *wife*, he sneered. "You one of her stupid nosy-bitch friends?"

"Actually, no," Kate said. "We're with the FBI. We're in town looking into a string of recent murders, and your name came up."

"Is that right?"

"It is. Seems that you might have had access to several of the homes we—"

Her words were halted as the man moved with blatant speed. In her long career, Kate had been trained to expect the unexpected—to always be prepared for anything. But even she had to take a few seconds for her mind to catch up to what was happening.

Redman slapped at the mug of beer he was drinking from. The action was so sudden and unexpected that Kate jumped, nearly falling from her barstool. The mug of beer came right at her, falling off the bar and splashing against her. The glass mug struck her knee and then hit the floor, where it shattered.

Reeling for balance, Kate looked back at DeMarco, as if to make sure someone else was seeing this absurd turn of events and she wasn't just imagining it. DeMarco looked just as confused as Kate was, her hand hovering hesitantly over her sidearm.

And that distraction was all it took. By the time Kate slid away from the barstool, smelling beer all over her, Redman was headed to the right, toward the restaurant's outdoor area.

Kate heard DeMarco yell out: *"Freeze!"*

It sounded almost as absurd as what had just happened to her. Kate took off after Redman, DeMarco right on her heels. She found herself reaching for her gun but knew better than to pull it out in a public place unless it was absolutely necessary.

She was only about five steps behind Redman when he blasted right through the door that led outside onto the little deck over the water that connected the two halves of the restaurant. Kate watched as he took a hard right, headed back toward the street. She and DeMarco ran through the door before it had time to close and took off after him.

Running had never bothered Kate; even at her age, she often enjoyed it. Of course, running down a potential suspect was much different from her morning runs through Carytown or some of the nature trails around Richmond. She and DeMarco were about equally fast, DeMarco pulling just slightly ahead as they gave chase. Kate saw that DeMarco had not pulled her weapon yet, either. Kate figured that a man who had come to drink away the failure of losing another job and trying to stay away from his wife was likely not packing any heat. But, of course, he was definitely running for *some* reason.

If Redman was drunk, it was not evident in the way he ran. There was urgency in his steps as he ran forward without looking back. He appeared to be going straight, which would eventually lead them to the little main stretch of road that served as Estes's Main Street, passing through town and running along the edge of the lake. But he took a very sudden left turn. For a moment, Kate thought the man had gotten confused (perhaps he was drunk after all) and was going to slam right into the side of a small drug store.

But as she and DeMarco neared the place where he turned, she saw the entrance to a small alleyway.

As DeMarco turned into the alley, Kate followed closely behind. They alley cut behind several businesses, ending in a chain-link fence. But just as the agents entered the alleyway, Kate saw Redman take another left, winding behind more buildings. If he knew the area as well as his speed indicated, she feared they might lose him.

They came to where Redman had taken the second left, following behind him. He had managed to gain a few feet on them, taking a bit more of a lead. Even now, as they entered the same alley—this one thinner and clearly used only for businesses to dump their trash for pickup—Redman was already nearing the end of it.

Here, he continued straight, heading for an opening that revealed a street at the end. Kate managed to find another gear somewhere in her calves and lungs. She took the lead over DeMarco, resisting the urge to pull her gun and fire a warning shot to freeze the man. And while she might get a pass from Duran over such an action, she knew it was would not be smart to use such a tactic in front of DeMarco. She knew it was never smart to fire a shot unless it was absolutely necessary—especially not midday in a quiet little lakeside town.

So instead, she simply ran on. She closed the distance between them as Redman neared the street. He hung a right and it was the sudden movement of it that helped Kate gain an advantage. She had to give him credit; he took the turn at the last minute, likely trying to get a few more steps on them.

But in doing so, his shoulder barely clipped the edge of the wall to his right. He bounced from it, missed about two steps, and then continued the turn. But by the time he had his balance and trajectory again, Kate was close enough. She dove low, knowing she no longer had the strength for a traditional tackle. Instead, she went for his knees. She drove her shoulders into the back of his knees, banging her own knees on the pavement as she did so.

The pain in her right leg was all the evidence she needed to remind her that she could not be as physical as she once could. The low blow was weak, only working because it caused Redman's feet to tangle together. He went down, instantly pulling himself away from her weak grip.

Kate hung on to his right leg, pulling back on it just as DeMarco played clean-up. She fell on him, placing a knee in the small of his back while she pulled his arms behind him and applied her handcuffs.

Kate rolled over into a sitting position, then slowly got to her feet. She was out of breath and her right knee was an electric knot of pain. She looked around and saw that a small crowd had watched it all go down. One of the bystanders was a young boy, watching things unfold with wide eyes and a huge smile.

"I don't enjoy running when I don't have to, Mr. Redman," DeMarco said as she hauled him up to his feet. She, too, had noticed the small crowd gathering around. With a rather embarrassed look on her face, she eyed Kate and asked: "You okay?"

"I will be. Just dinged my knee pretty bad."

This was true, of course. But the little spike of pain that refused to go away had her slightly worried. She'd injured the same knee while on duty in her thirties—nothing serious, just a little sprain and tear—and she thought it possible she had aggravated the old injury.

DeMarco gave her an uncertain look, as if she wasn't buying it. But she said nothing. She only gave Redman a little nudge, pointing him in the direction of the area where they had parked the car.

"Come on, Mr. Redman," DeMarco said. "Let's head to the police station and have a little talk."

DeMarco ushered him on while Kate walked on behind, doing her best to hide the slight limp as she walked.

CHAPTER TWENTY

Sheriff Armstrong did not seem all that surprised to see Matt Redman being led into the station. She was on the phone when Kate and DeMarco entered; Kate could hear her speaking to someone about getting a police record on one of the agents who worked for Crest Realty. Armstrong finished up the call as quickly as she could and then fell in behind the agents as they marched Redman down the hall toward the interrogation room.

"Jimmy!" Armstrong yelled, calling to what Kate was starting to assume was the most reliable officer on the Estes PD other than Armstrong herself. "Pull the file on Matt Redman and bring it to interrogation."

A faint *"On it"* came in response from elsewhere in the building.

Together, the three women filed into the interrogation room. Redman didn't have to be asked to take a seat; he seemed to be familiar with the scenario. He slowly made his way behind the tale and when he sat down in the chair, he did so with a hateful glare cast toward them.

"It's been a while, Mr. Redman," Armstrong said, glaring right back at him.

"He a regular?" DeMarco asked.

"He was for a while. But he hasn't graced this station with his presence in about two years now. He's on probation for assault, if my memory serves correct. You want to fill in the facts, Mr. Redman?"

"You'd love that, huh?" he asked. He then stared down Kate and DeMarco. "My ex-girlfriend and I got drunk one night a few years ago. Got into an argument and I hit her. Twice. I'm not proud of it, but it happened. But in small towns like this, it's just as bad as murder. It sticks with you. You're a woman abuser for life."

"And the petty theft?" Armstrong added. "You want to tell them about that, too?"

"I paid that fine," Redman spat.

"Doesn't mean it wipes it from your record."

As if on cue, a knock came to the door and Jimmy stepped in. He handed a file folder out, insure of who to hand it to. Kate took it and opened it up, finding three forms and a photograph of the right brow of Matt Redman's ex-girlfriend. It appeared that at least one of the punches he'd thrown had been a powerful one. She checked out the forms and handed the folder over to DeMarco.

The stealing changes were indeed minor…at first. Just petty theft: stealing inexpensive tools and pipe work from construction sites in the area. But, given the locales of the recent murders, that type of theft actually meant much more. Kate found herself looking at Redman's shoulders and arms. He did not have the build of a huge man, but he had biceps and shoulders that told the tale of years of manual labor.

He'd certainly be strong enough to haul a woman up by her neck with the use of a makeshift noose.

"Want to tell us why you recently lost your job with Mulligan Movers?" Kate asked.

"I didn't *lose* it," Redman said. "I quit."

"Any reason why?"

"Because Jack—the owner—is a dick. He didn't pay enough."

"He described you as being a hard worker."

"I am a hard worker."

"Not *too* hard," DeMarco said. "The way we hear it, you've quit three jobs in the past year or so."

Listening to DeMarco, Kate started to stitch together something of a profile. And with each stitch she placed along the seams, the more promising of a suspect Matt Redman became. He did not stay at one job for very long and he had a history of stealing from job sites. More often than not, this indicated that he likely stole from the people he worked for and then moved on before his transgressions were discovered. More than that, his work history gave him at least a rudimentary knowledge of how homes were built and sold.

"It's all shit work, that's why," Redman said.

"Maybe you'd find better work if you stuck with an employer for more than a few months," DeMarco commented.

It was clear that Redman wanted to say a number of things to DeMarco, but he showed restraint. His hands were clasped together in front of him, still handcuffed together.

"Mr. Redman, were you stealing anything from Mr. Mulligan before you quit?" Kate asked.

"I'm not answering that."

"There's no reason not to," DeMarco said. "We're questioning you on the grounds of having access to at least two of the homes that people have recently been killed in. I could give two shits if you were stealing from Mulligan."

Kate bit back a wince; she wished DeMarco hadn't gone so extreme on that. If Redman was smart enough (and that was a big *if*), he might figure out that they had no intention of pressing charges. And if he *wasn't* the killer, that would give him the upper hand. If he *knew* they had nothing on him, it could make for a very difficult interrogation.

But apparently, Redman wasn't that smart. Maybe DeMarco had already noted this and banked on it. Perhaps, Kate thought, she was not giving DeMarco enough credit.

"I wasn't stealing from Mulligan. But yeah ... I had taken a few things from the properties we worked, moving furniture in. But not from Mulligan. Not yet, anyway. But I had planned on it. Almost did it last night, even though I'd already quit. But I decided to go out drinking instead. It just wasn't worth the trouble."

"What had you planned on stealing?" Kate asked. It occurred to her as she stood there that she still smelled like whatever beer Redman had spilled on her. She knew it was a bit immature of her to think so, but it made her hope Redman *was* the killer just so she could see the look on his face when he realized he was trapped.

And he might very well be the killer, Kate thought. *The pieces we have on him are all rather small, but they fit perfectly together to make a much larger picture.*

"Nothing big. Copper pipes, some flex pipe, steel rods. Things like that. Nothing the construction guys would miss. The shit just sits there on the sites for weeks and weeks, you know?"

"Then why steal them?" Armstrong asked.

He looked at them as if they were idiots. For a moment, Kate didn't think he was going to answer. "The small-time builders a few towns over will buy that stuff. These are the companies that hire the Mexican guys that hang out in front of Lowe's or Home Depot looking for carpentry work, you know? Saves them some money."

"Sounds like you know a lot about it," Kate said. "You done it before?"

"Yeah, it's part of the petty theft charge." He seemed to understand that he had also just confessed to reselling the stolen goods. It was the look of a man who had been running a race and realized that he had just stepped in a pile of dog droppings.

DeMarco stared him down for a while. Kate let her have the floor, wondering where she was headed with it. It was clear that Matt Redman was not the brightest man in Estes, and DeMarco had already proven that in terms of conversation, he wasn't very observant.

That, or he's nervous as hell, Kate thought. *Maybe he does have something to hide. Maybe he's so willing to tell us about his plans to steal building materials because he's hoping it will distract from something much worse.*

"Mr. Redman, I'm going to show you three addresses," DeMarco said, rifling through a stack of papers on the table. "I need you to tell me if you have worked in or around them in the past week. It makes no sense to lie because we can have it checked by Jack Mulligan and the other men you've been working with."

That said, DeMarco slid him a printout with the three addresses where the real estate agents had been killed. The paper also had a few details about the murders, but DeMarco had covered that up with a folded sheet of paper. Redman looked them over and started nodding almost instantly.

"All three of them," he said. He looked up to them as he said this, his eyes narrowing. It appeared he was being very cautious, trying to gauge their reaction to his response. Kate could see that he did indeed appear to feel trapped now. She'd seen it before in countless sets of eyes from behind the interrogation table—darting pupils, the narrowing and squinting of the eyes, looking around the room in a paranoid state.

"How recently?" Kate asked.

"I don't know. Maybe a week or so."

"Do you have access to the home you work around or do you need your employers to let you in?" Kate asked.

It was a bait question, and one that Redman took right away. Kate knew it was a question that he would be emphatic over if he was truthful, or cautious about if he was lying. And as he answered, she could see him focusing, perhaps trying to see all the ways he could be found out, wondering if there were trails they could pick up if they kept seeking. But his answer was already out and the *oh-shit* that briefly flashed across his face told Kate all she needed to know.

"I have access," he said, then hesitated as that wary look came across his face. "But, you know, I need permission first."

Kate could see DeMarco preparing to ask another question. She reached out and gently touched DeMarco's elbow. When DeMarco looked back, Kate gave her a simple shake of the head.

"Mr. Redman, thanks for all this," Kate said. "Sit tight, and we'll get you out of here soon. Agent DeMarco, can I see you out in the hallway for a moment?"

When DeMarco turned toward her, Kate was relieved to see the look of understanding on her face. It was another way they were growing close as partners; DeMarco knew most of what Kate had just said was bullshit. She just needed to throw something by her partner while not standing in front of their suspect.

They walked into the hallway, with Armstrong trailing behind them. They took a few steps away from the door and spoke in voices just above a whisper.

"He's lying about something," DeMarco said.

"I agree," Kate said. "But as we sit there talking to him, it's becoming clear to me that right now, there's really one better place to get answers. He's being forthcoming for the most part, but he's also being shady."

"You thinking we need to go back and speak to his wife?" DeMarco asked.

"That's exactly what I'm thinking. Now that we know enough about some of his past crimes, I think his wife would be more than happy to spill more on him."

"That's Henrietta Redman," Armstrong said. "Sort of along the same lines of Regina Voss—juts a grade-A snake. Of course, given the nature of the man she married, I guess she has a reason."

"Yes, we already spoke to her briefly today," Kate said. "She seems to be pissed at Matt. If we strike now, there's no telling how much help she might be."

"Let's be quick, then," DeMarco said. "Sheriff, do you mind sitting by here with Redman while we go speak to his wife again?"

"Yeah, I can handle that. Let me know if you need anything else."

Kate and DeMarco headed for the front of the building. Kate could feel that familiar stirring of excitement of a case coming close to it end. But it was slightly muted by two other things: that her clothes still reeked of beer and that the pain in her right knee seemed to be going nowhere and she was pretty sure it was swelling.

CHAPTER TWENTY ONE

Kate typically hated working on cases where there were a lot of circles—going back and forth to points already discovered and investigated. But the instincts she had come to rely on throughout her career seemed to feel quite all right with heading back to Matt Redman's apartment to visit with his wife. She felt even better about it when they saw the look of absolute joy on Henrietta Redman's face when they told her they needed to ask even more questions about her husband.

"Look," Henrietta said as she led them into her small living room. It was remarkably tidy, perhaps because Henrietta had been putting her energy into cleaning while waiting to find out the fate of her husband. "I love the jerk and all, but I kept telling him that one of these days, his past was going to catch up to him. Matt has always been stubborn. He doesn't learn lessons and he has never learned from his mistakes. And he has made a lot of them."

"What can you tell us about his criminal record?" Kate asked. "Was that before or during your marriage?"

"Both. Stupid stuff, too. Stealing from worksites. And before me, he was busted for beating up on his ex-girlfriend."

"This latest strong of events—with him quitting this job with Mulligan Movers—it doesn't seem to surprise you. You seem sort of done with it all."

"Well, yeah! Wouldn't you be? He keeps telling me he's going to try to clean himself up but then doesn't want to work. He's even talked about trying some stupid online scam stuff just to make some quick money. Now...don't get me wrong; when Matt works, he works *hard*. He can be a good worker...when he wants to be. But he's always looking for a shortcut, you know? That's how he got busted for stealing building supplies and furniture."

"Have you ever wondered if he'd do something worse?" DeMarco asked. "Something beyond simple theft?"

The question seemed to surprise Henrietta, and the expression that crossed her face was all the answer Kate needed. Still, Henrietta also gave a verbal answer.

"Sometimes," she said. "He could have. A bad day at work or just be in one of his drunk rages and I always think about what he did to that ex-girlfriend of his. He can get so damned mean."

"Over what, exactly?" DeMarco asked.

"Everything. But, more than anything, he hates how the properties around Estes are bought and sold for these expensive homes. He's always felt it wasn't fair that contractors and real estate companies make so much money, while he makes barely over minimum wage."

Maybe that would be different if he'd stick with a job and stop stealing materials, Kate thought. But that was neither here nor there; what she was hearing was more motivation for someone like Matt Redman to snap.

"Do you know if he'd stolen anything as of late?" DeMarco asked.

"I have no idea. He sort of keeps to himself."

"Has he been acting any different lately?" Kate inquired. "Maybe being more secretive than usual?"

"Yeah, a little. But I didn't think anything of it." She started to get suspicious for the first time and now eyed them with something like fear. "Is he...Jesus, do you think he could have really...?"

"We aren't sure right now," Kate said, though she was becoming more and more certain that he *had* done something—perhaps something irreparably bad. "Right now, we're just trying to put together as much information as we can."

"Mrs. Redman," DeMarco said, "is there any place in the apartment or maybe something he keeps close to him that he did his best to keep hidden from you?"

"Nothing serious, no. He's got some porn videos on his laptop he pretends I don't know about. And he's got this strange fixation with this old lunch pail he takes to work. It's a hand-me-down from his father. He's very protective of it."

"Do you know where it is?" Kate asked.

"It's usually in his truck. But he brought it in last night and put it in the coat closet just down the hall. Made the comment that he probably wouldn't need it anymore for a while since he was out of work."

"You mind if we have a look at it?" Kate asked.

"Sure ... one second."

Henrietta Redman exited the living room and walked into the small adjoined hallway. She opened up the closet, knelt down, and withdrew an old silver lunch pail. It did indeed look old and Kate had no problem imagining it once belonging to Matt Redman's father. It had the dents and additional wear and tear along its surface to support its age.

Henrietta brought it over and handed it to Kate. Kate wasn't even sure what she was looking for as she looked at the small latch that kept it closed. She thumbed it open and pulled the lid back. It made a very soft squeaking noise and she pushed the top open. She and DeMarco looked inside together and saw nothing more than an empty lunch pail.

It unfolded almost like a small fishing tacklebox. Only, the top part was totally removable from the track. It came free with a gentle nudge, which surprised Kate, given how old the thing was. She peered into the hidden bottom section of the pail and found it just as empty as the top.

"Kate ..."

DeMarco was looking to the top tray Kate had removed. More precisely, she was looking *under* it.

Kate lifted it and took a few seconds to study what she saw there. There were five keys, all taped to the bottom of the tray with thin gray strips of duct tape. Each piece of tape contained a single word, scrawled in small handwriting with what looked like magic marker.

The word on the first piece, holding the first key, was **Brewington**. The word on the second key was **Leander**. While Kate had no idea what Brewington was (though she was assuming it was a street somewhere in Estes), Leander was familiar. So was the word on the fourth key: **Hammermill**.

"Mrs. Redman, do you have any idea what we're looking at here?" Kate asked.

Henrietta shook her head, just as shocked by the discovery as the agents sitting in her living room.

"Any reason why he'd be hiding these keys?" Kate asked, already heading back for the front door.

"No. I don't... I don't know. It doesn't make sense..."

"We're going to need to take these keys, okay?" DeMarco asked.

"Yeah, sure. Just... what has he done? What has Matt done?"

"We don't know yet," Kate said, though she was pretty certain she *did* know. She was so certain that these keys were the smoking gun that she had nearly managed to look beyond the pain in her knee. If these hidden keys meant what she thought they did, she felt like this case might be wrapped within an hour or so.

"We'll keep you posted, though," DeMarco said, joining Kate on her hurried trip to the front door.

"Don't bother," Henrietta said with quite a bit of anger in her voice. "If he's done something bad, I don't care if he *never* comes back."

That's a good thing, Kate thought. *Because the way it's looking, there's a very good chance he won't.*

Leander Drive was the closest location to the Redman residence, so that's where DeMarco was heading while Kate called Armstrong to fill her in. She requested that she send officers out to the three streets that were not currently known as the sites of murders while she and DeMarco checked Leander and Hammermill.

"No addresses?" Armstrong asked.

"Nothing full, no," Kate said. "Just street names. We need to know the addresses of any available homes on those three streets, as well as the real estate agency that has them listed. If we can then connect Mulligan Movers or even just Matt Redman to any of them, that could be the entire case."

"I'll get it started right now," Armstrong said with excitement in her voice. She had taken two of the keys before leaving the precinct, doing what she could to cut down their time. "Stay tuned."

Kate ended the call and stared ahead through the windshield as DeMarco sped them toward Leander, which was less than two miles away from the apartment complex the Redmans resided in.

"You want to tell me what's wrong with your leg?" DeMarco asked out of the blue.

"What do you mean?" Kate asked.

"You're limping. You're trying to hide it, but I noticed it as we were leaving Henrietta Redman. Was it during the chase out of the restaurant?"

"Yeah," Kate said, not seeing the point in lying.

"Just a tweak or something worse?"

"I think it's just a tweak. Maybe I pulled something. Really, it's okay."

While the pain *had* subsided a bit within the past fifteen minutes or so, it was still there. And because she had injured the area before, she thought it might be more than a simple pull. But she could still walk and the pain wasn't nearly bad enough to affect her performance. So, for right now, she had to push it away.

"Any theories on the keys?" Kate asked before DeMarco could ask more questions about her leg.

"Sure. I think he somehow got a copy of the keys as he worked moving jobs. Not sure why, though. Unless, of course, Redman is indeed the killer. Having keys to the properties he intended to kill the agents in would certainly make it much easier to get to them."

"I'm thinking the same thing. The question, though, is where is the key to the property on Magnolia?"

"Maybe he had more hiding spots for keys. Right now, I'm more concerned about what he might have planned for those other three keys. Or, rather, what Armstrong and her officers might be about to find."

It was a harrowing thought, and one that sat heavy on Kate's mind until DeMarco pulled the car into the driveway of the property on Leander Drive, the same vacant and newly furnished home where Bea Faraday had been killed. Kate plucked the Leander key from the underside of the lunch pail tray as DeMarco parked. They raced to the front porch and even before Kate tried sliding the key into the front door lock, she had a feeling—a *sense*—of what would happen.

So, when the key slid perfectly into the lock, she was not at all surprised. Just to make absolutely sure, she turned the key and then tried the doorknob. The door opened easily onto the foyer and the still-stale smell of a recent crime scene.

"For the sake of consistency," DeMarco said, "I suppose we should also try the house on Hammermill."

"I was thinking the same thing," Kate said. "And if that key fits … I think we can officially arrest Matt Redman for three murders."

They quickly exited the house, locked up behind themselves, and ran back to the car. No more than twenty seconds passed after DeMarco pulled away from the curb before her phone rang.

"It's Armstrong," she said, answering the call and placing it on speaker mode. "This is DeMarco," she said.

"Agent DeMarco, I thought you'd want to know that we have confirmation on the Brewington key. It opens the front door to a house currently for sale. We entered the home, though, and found nothing out of the ordinary."

Maybe that one was supposed to be next on his list, Kate thought.

Apparently, DeMarco had been thinking the same thing. "We have to assume the keys to homes that were not murder sites could have been next on his list," she said. "We've just confirmed that the key marked Leander unlocked the home Bea Faraday was killed in. We're headed over to Hammermill now."

"So, it's him, isn't it?" Armstrong asked.

"I'm not ready to chisel it in stone just yet," DeMarco said, "but it certainly does seem like it."

Again, it was another beat where Kate and DeMarco were on the same page. Kate glared out of the window, knowing that Hammermill must be checked out just for the sake of protocol. But with every second that passed, she started to grow anxious, feeling that the man who had killed three real estate agents was currently sitting in the interrogation room of the Estes Police Department, guilty as hell and already captured.

Chapter Twenty Two

The key that had been marked Hammermill did indeed unlock the door to the Hammermill murder scene. Once Kate had DeMarco confirmed this, they reconvened back at the police station, where Matt Redman was officially placed under arrest for the murders of Tamara Bateman, Dhayna Tsui, and Bea Faraday.

Kate watched Redman closely as Armstrong recited the charges against him, as well as his rights. He looked puzzled and clearly taken off guard. She'd seen many guilty parties attempt both looks at the same time and it usually came off as looking comical. But for just a moment, Matt Redman looked as if he had no idea where he was. He looked like he had just woken up in some place he had never been before, his brain trying its best to make sense of the situation.

Kate did not like that look. It appeared too genuine. Still, though, his arguments against the charges were pretty much non-existent. He simply stared at them, dumbfounded, and was finally able to get out a single question.

"The fuck are you talking about?"

And even then, at the end of the question, there was a degree of helplessness to his voice. It was not the sort of thing that could be faked very well.

Kate slowly made her way out of the room, with DeMarco on her heels. "It feels right," DeMarco said. "He even looks guilty now that we've dropped the charges on him."

"He does," Kate admitted. But the look on his face had her second-guessing herself. It was not a great way to feel as she watched

DeMarco place a call to Duran. She knew what DeMarco was doing; she was letting Duran know that they had a killer—mainly so Duran could then contact the governor so he'd stop breathing down the bureau's neck.

Kate walked back into the small conference room they had been using as HQ. She looked at all of the notes on the dry-erase board, and the scattered papers on the desk. She sat down at the desk, stretching out her right leg. The knee was getting sore, the pain lessening but the effects of the injury starting to settle in. She tested the area with her fingers, finding nothing out of place, but tenderness throughout.

"I'm going to *make* you see a doctor for that."

She turned around and saw DeMarco standing in the doorway. Slowly, she entered the room and closed the door behind her. "I've seen you like this before, you know."

"Like what?"

"Worried that we're not done even though it looks like we are," DeMarco said, sitting down across from her. "And when I did see you like this, you turned out to be right. So what is it? About half an hour ago, you seemed to be comfortable with the idea that Matt Redman was our killer. But your expression and attitude make me think you've changed your mind."

"I wouldn't say I've changed my mind," Kate said. "But did you see his reaction when Armstrong dropped the charges on him? He was legitimately shocked. I've seen suspects try to fake that look before. Some are quite good, but it still comes off as unauthentic."

"Having those keys, though..."

"Yes, I know. But still, if we dig a bit deeper, is that really enough? I mean, we know he has a history of stealing things. What better way to break into a home to steal things than with a key?"

"So you think him having keys for two of the murder scenes is just a coincidence?" DeMarco asked, clearly surprised.

"I don't know. But I'm willing to at least consider it as a coincidence. Think about it," she said, well aware that she was now merely thinking out loud, putting her own thoughts into order as she sifted through all of them. "We know that he feels the people he has worked for were money-hungry. And the builders and contractors, too. Henrietta did say he also resented the real estate agencies, but nothing so strong that it would drive him to *kill* real estate agents. If he had a point to prove through murder, wouldn't it make more sense to go after the men he had once worked for—or even the builders?"

"It could be his messed up way of ensuring the costs and values of the homes dropped a bit," DeMarco pointed out.

Kate nodded, as it was a very good point. But even then, all of that did not fit the MO of a man who had, so far, committed nothing worse that petty theft and situational domestic abuse.

"If anything, though," Kate said, "Redman having those keys really only supports his old chargers of theft. Of course, it also makes him a very likely suspect to the murders but... I don't know. It just doesn't feel *right*."

She watched DeMarco's face as she took all of this in. Slowly, little seeds of doubt started to work their way into her expression, most notably at the corners of her mouth, where a very small frown was starting to form.

"Shit," DeMarco said. She shrugged and sighed, leaning forward in her seat. "Well, if nothing else, we have an arrest on the records. Even if we're wrong, it buys us a ton of time with the governor. But Kate... I can't just assume we're wrong on this. I mean... if not Redman, then who?"

"I don't know," she said.

But as she said that, an image popped up in her mind. She saw an old car, a man sitting inside of it—parked in front of a house that was for sale. She had started speaking to him for just a moment before she had been interrupted by the shouting match between Regina Voss, DeMarco, and some other local woman.

She hadn't forgotten about the car or the man behind the wheel, but in the pursuit of Matt Redman, the car and its owner *had* become much less of a talking point.

What was that man doing there anyway? she wondered. She tried to recall the scant conversation she'd had with him but it was faint at best. She thought it might be worth making a call to see if they could pull the records for all black Tauruses in the area. It would be a needle in a haystack sort of search because she wasn't sure what year the model had been, so they'd have to go back pretty far. She wondered if it would even be worth it.

Before she could latch onto it, there was a knock on the door. Armstrong opened the door and stepped inside with an apologetic look on her face. "Sorry," she said. "Am I interrupting anything?"

"Not at all," Kate said. "What do you need?"

"I thought you'd want to know that I just got off of the phone with the governor. He's asked me to send over a report that he can use for a television news announcement. He also wants to know if the lead agent on the case is going to be available to be a part of it."

"So he's assembling a press conference?" Kate asked.

"In my opinion, yes. But he was very careful to not call it that."

Kate grinned at DeMarco. "Like it or not, you're the lead agent. So you have fun with that."

Kate was happy to see that there was some excitement in DeMarco's face. Kate knew it would be the first time the younger agent had been tasked with such responsibility—the first time her contributions to a case would be noticed by the public in any capacity. She was a good agent and as far as Kate was concerned, she deserved the attention.

Armstrong, meanwhile, seemed as if she was out of her element. She looked like she had wandered into a room she had never seen before and though she wanted to help, she wasn't sure where to pitch in. Kate wondered what her own thoughts were on the charges they had brought against Redman now that he had officially been arrested.

"Well, you have fun with the governor," Kate said, playfully slapping DeMarco on the leg. She got up and started for the door where Armstrong was still standing, as if in some sort of daze.

"Where are you going?" DeMarco asked.

"Just to check on something."

"Kate … if Redman isn't our guy and we make this big announcement on television and to the papers …"

"I know. But maybe it won't come to that."

"What's going on?" Armstrong said.

"Agent Wise is having second thoughts on the arrest of Matt Redman," DeMarco said with as much good nature as she could muster.

"What?"

"It's nothing to worry about right now," Kate said. "You go on here as usual, as if we know for certain Redman is our man. I just want to follow up on a few things."

Armstrong looked at both of them with some concern and then finally gave a nod before leaving the room. When she was gone, DeMarco looked to Kate and put as much intensity into her stare as she could.

"You're not going to do anything stupid, are you?"

"No."

"How's the knee?"

"It hurts a little. Sore. But I won't be running or anything like that. I just want to check out one of the properties … the one I was looking into right before you got to experience the wrath of Regina Voss."

"And then what?"

Kate wasn't thrilled with how intimately DeMarco was grilling her, but she understood it. This was *her* case; she was the lead and she wanted to make sure every loose end was tied up and everything was taken care of. Having her partner wandering off on the verge of a press conference following an arrest would no doubt be making her uneasy.

"And then I'll be back. I may try to talk to the agent representing the home, but that'll be all."

"Okay. Just … please try to be back in time for the press conference. The idea of standing up in front of live mics and cameras makes me nervous as hell."

"I'll do my best," Kate said. "Thanks, DeMarco. You've done well here."

DeMarco had time to only smile before Kate left the room. Kate let that smile sit on her mind for a while. She was beyond proud of DeMarco. Given enough time and tutelage, she was going to be an incredibly proficient agent—maybe with a career to rival her own. It made Kate want to stay true to her word, of getting back to the station before the flurry of lights and cameras showed up.

Kate made her way to the parking lot and got into the car she and DeMarco had been sharing for the last few days. She reached into the back seat for the folder they had kept most of their files and notes in, pulling out the list of available properties for sale in the Estes area. She scanned the list for the house in question— a five-hundred-thousand-dollar listing on Duffey Street—and was momentarily struck with a terrible bit of foreshadowing when she saw that Tamara Bateman's name was listed as representing it.

Kate pulled out her phone and called Lakeside Realty. She thought the male vice that answered sounded familiar. "Lakeside Realty."

"Is this Mr. Towers?" she asked.

"It is. How can I help you?"

"This is Agent Wise. I'm looking at the list of available properties in Estes again and noticed that Tamara Bateman was listed as representing the house located at 517 Duffey Street. I was wondering who might have picked that up."

"That would be me, actually," Brett Towers said.

"You think you have time to meet me out there?" Kate asked. "I'm working on a hunch here and would like to get inside."

"Yeah, I think I can manage that. Can you give me half an hour?"

"Sure. If you can make it faster, though, I'd appreciate it."

"I'll see what I can do."

They ended the call as Kate pulled out of the police station parking lot. The day was reaching its end and she had no idea how long it would be before the news crews started to descend on Estes.

But she figured giving Brett Towers half an hour wasn't going to be the end of the world. With that in mind, she turned her car in the direction of Duffey Street. The closer she got, the more clearly she could see that battered old car and the seemingly innocent man sitting inside of it.

And the clearer that image got, the more certain she became that in all of the commotion with Regina Voss on the street, she may have allowed something to slip through the cracks.

CHAPTER TWENTY THREE

She arrived at 517 Duffey Street fourteen minutes after leaving the police department. The car she had seen yesterday was not there. In fact, there were no cars parked along the street for a fairly good stretch of space. As Kate parked, she noticed another house farther down the street that was also for sale.

If houses for sale were somehow part of the killer's motive, she sure had a hell of a whole lot to choose from in Estes, she thought.

She got out of the car and walked to the front porch. She was not at all surprised to find the door locked. The little lock box with the key inside sat just to the right of the door. As she observed it, it occurred to her that Matt Redman's little stash of keys had not hidden one for a property on Duffey Street.

Curious, Kate left the porch and walked around to the back. She could tell the house was relatively new, though not an entirely new build. Still, the siding had recently been power washed and she was pretty sure the planted shrubs that ran halfway along the sides were all new and refurbished. She walked to the back of the house and looked across the large backyard. A flower garden sat along the back fence, as well as a strip of dirt sprouting something that she thought looked like dying tomato vines.

She came to the edge of an expansive back porch. Before climbing the stirs, though, she crossed a small cement patch that ran beneath the porch; it was a secondary patio of sorts, complete with an outdoor sofa and glass table. She tried the door there, apparently leading to a downstairs area. It, too, was locked.

She finally walked up the porch steps onto the gorgeous back deck. Like the siding, it had recently been cleaned. She saw that there were actually two entrance points to the deck—one through a set of sliding glass doors to the far right of the deck and then a doorway on the left. The door contained two thin windows, sitting adjacent to one another. Kate peered through the glass and saw a sparkling clean kitchen on the other side.

She tried the door and then the sliding glass doors, finding them all locked. She shrugged to herself, figuring it wouldn't hurt her to wait ten more minutes for Brett Towers. She came down the stairs and started back around the other side of the house. At the back corner, a few plain shrubs had been planted.

And if not for the peculiar indentation in the side of one of the shrubs, she may have completely ignored the window that sat just above it. It looked as if something had fallen into it from the back or that it had been disturbed some other way. She walked to it, her instinct telling her that it wasn't so much the shrub that she should be interested, but the window. She walked behind the shrub and looked at the window.

At first glance, the window was closed. But then she saw the scuff marks right around the corner of the frame. The window was installed low enough where she could see it clearly. The top of the window was over her head, but the bottom was about chest-high. She placed her palms on either side of the window and pushed upward as hard as she could. In doing so, she found that her hunch was correct; the dents in the shrubbery, the scuff marks along the bottom of the window—it all indicated that someone had jimmied the window open and crawled inside.

The window went up with a slight sliding noise. Kate found herself staring into what appeared to be just some small extra room—maybe an office or a study of some kind. There was no furniture, just carpet and a basic light hanging in the center of the ceiling.

She knew the logical thing to do would be to take note of it and wait for Towers. But she also knew that she had a very anxious partner back at the police station, waiting for her to return as soon as she could. She thought about the evidence they'd found of squatters in two of the crime scenes and wondered if she'd find something similar inside this house.

If the jimmied window was any indication, she was pretty sure she would.

Feeling only a little silly, Kate placed her hands inside the opened window, bracing herself against the frame. She pulled herself slightly up, to where her feet weren't touching the ground, and slid inside. There was nothing graceful about it, and she nearly fell on her head when she made her way inside. In the end, she ended up partially falling into the house on her right side, once again dinging her injured knee.

She sat there, pressed against the wall, for a moment. She took out her phone and texted DeMarco the address where she was, adding: **Back window to property jimmied open. I'm inside to check it out.**

Kate quietly got to her feet and walked to the room's only doorway. The door was open, revealing what appeared to be a downstairs den—the sort of area that might make a good man cave or craft area for a thrifty type. A single couch sat against the far wall. There was no way Kate could be sure, but she thought it was new. She thought of Matt Redman and some other movers working their way through the home, setting furniture up and opening up the spaces.

She stepped out into the room and looked around. There was no evidence of anyone having squatted here, though it would have been difficult unless the person had left anything behind. She made her way through the room, heading to the left side where a set of stairs led up to the main floor.

Taking the stairs as quietly as she could, Kate realized that the house itself was eerily quiet. There was not even the ambient hum of an air conditioner or a running refrigerator. As she focused on that quiet, looking for anything at all that might indicate movement elsewhere in the house, she realized that she could hear her own breathing as she neared the top of the stairs.

The stairway came to an end just off of the foyer upstairs. Another set was directly beside her, going up into the second floor. She peered up those stairs but did not take them. Instead, she moved through the foyer and into the house. The area where the foyer and living room met was a wide open space, highlighted by an absolutely stunning chandelier hanging from the high ceiling.

The house was an open-floor plan, the foyer, living room, den area, and dining room all joined together. The kitchen was the only room that seemed to occupy its own space, separated from the rest of the area by a long bar.

She took a step deeper into the house and nearly screamed when her phone chimed at her. She slapped at her pocket, embarrassed that she had been so frightened of the noise of an incoming text. As she pulled the phone out, she was also embarrassed that she had failed to put it on silent mode upon entering the house. If there *was* anyone hiding away somewhere else within the home, she had just given herself away.

She saw that the incoming text was from DeMarco. It was a simple **OK** in response to the text she had sent earlier. She slipped the phone back into her pocket and continued on into the house. By the time she reached the kitchen area, she felt foolish for having climbed in through the window downstairs. Yes, the scrapes on the window and the fact that it had been unlocked was proof that someone had broken in, but had she really been expecting to find a squatter just hanging out in the house? Had she *really* been expecting to come across the man who had killed three women, idly wasting his time away in what might have been the scene for one of his future murders?

Kate stood by the kitchen counter and sighed. She checked her watch and saw that she had a little less than ten minutes before Brett Towers was scheduled to arrive. And really, that was just a waste of time; she'd only needed him to show up so he could unlock the front door for her.

You've overthought something again, she thought, scolding herself. *You have a very likely suspect back at the police department. Were you really too disappointed with how you came upon finding him? Did tweaking your right knee not provide enough of a thrill for you?*

The voice that scolded her belonged to Allen. But she could also hear Melissa in there, too. And buried under it all was another looming suspicion—one she did not want to face but had known was there from the moment she had arrived in Estes.

Are you that *determined to crack a case where DeMarco was assigned as lead? Do you really want to take that from her?*

Of course she didn't. And with that thought in mind, she pulled out her phone and sent a text to Brett Towers. **Sorry to be a pain, but scratch the visit to Duffey Street. Sorry if you're already out and on your way.**

She took a final look around the large open area of the first floor and started back for the stairs. She figured she'd go back out the window downstairs. She's take a picture and send it to Towers, just so he would know.

And after that, she'd head back to the station and do what she could to support DeMarco. She wanted to be there to celebrate closing the case—to help her through the potential minefield of a televised news conference. And after all of that, when she had returned home, she'd go to the doctor and see what was going on with her knee. Because as she walked back to the stairs, the pain started to come back, flaring up and radiating up her leg.

She was so focused on her knee and trying not to apply to much pressure on it that she missed the very brief shadow that momentarily fell across the floor in front of her. And it was that bit of inattention that caused all of the trouble that followed.

CHAPTER TWENTY FOUR

He was dreaming of his mother again. For the past few weeks, he'd been afraid to go to sleep because he knew there would be a dream of his mother waiting for him. He enjoyed seeing her in the dreams, but it was painful to wake up and realize she was no longer there. In the dreams, she looked beautiful. Her face was flawless and unmarred by the car accident that had taken her life. The last time he had physically seen her was in a hospital bed, kept alive by the machines surrounding the bed. The right side of her face had been partially burned, her right eye swollen shut and charred. Her jaw had also been dislocated, set in a way that made it look as if she were perpetually angry.

But in the dreams, she was perfect. She could smile at him and both of her ice-blue eyes would regard him with patience and love.

"What have I told you about being nice to the other kids in school?" she asked him in this most recent dream.

"To be kind," he answered.

"That's right. Now...what you've been doing...is that very nice?"

"No. But I had to. Mom, I had to do it."

"And why is that?"

He knew the answers but could not state them in the dream. It was as if these dreams were his mother's own private dominion and he could not do or say anything in these dreams that would upset her. And he was fine with that.

In the dream, they were standing in a perfectly empty house. The floors had been put down in the living room and the tile had

154

been set in the kitchen. There was no furniture yet. The walls still smelled like paint and the windows were new and sparkling. The entire house was bathed in perfect sunlight, casting their long shadows across the bare floors.

"I think it's time you stop now, Dougie," his mother said.

She'd called him that even up until he day she had died. He was twenty-eight and she had still called him that. He hated it and loved it all at the same time.

"I can't," he said. "It just makes me so mad, Mom. It makes me so mad and I can't stop. I can't help it." He squinted against the glare of the sun through the large kitchen window and added: "Is there something wrong with me?"

His mother opened her mouth to answer but a voice did not come out. Instead, it was an electronic sort of beeping noise that he heard.

"Mom?"

Dougie's eyes sprang open and he found himself looking at the ceiling of an upstairs bedroom.

That noise from his mother's mouth had not been from the dream. It had come from somewhere close by...somewhere inside the house.

He sat up, noticing that the sunlight coming in through the bedroom window was faded. He peered outside and saw that it was nearing dusk. He'd been asleep for several hours then; he wondered if the agent had already come and gone—if the agent had come at all. Ever since the FBI had shown up in town, there seemed to have been some sort of freeze on all real estate proceedings.

Well, someone *is downstairs right now,* he thought. *That dinging noise was from a cell phone.*

He supposed it could be the agent. From what he had put together, there was an agent due to arrive at this home in the next day or so. Of course, things had slowed down over the last day or so. And even if things were normal, he knew that any agent who might be here at such an hour—about half an hour away from dark falling outside—they'd be with a potential client. And if that was the case, he was going to have to get creative just to get out of this one.

He got to his feet, figuring he may as well go down to see who was there.

As he stood, he grabbed the piece of lumber he had brought in with him earlier in the day. It was slightly dented and had dried blood on it.

He also gathered up the length of rope he had brought in with him. He'd spied the chandelier downstairs. It was massive and, from what he could tell, could likely hold quite a bit of weight. It had been installed with industrial bolts, indicating some heavy installation equipment hidden within the ceiling.

He snuck out of the room and made his way down the hallway as quietly as he could. For a moment, he thought he was being followed. He turned to check behind him, nearly expecting to see his mother walking alongside him. But of course, she wasn't there. She had been buried in the same graveyard as his father, laid to rest a little over five months ago.

As he walked to the stairs, he remembered her fondly. He remembered her wanting to make a better life for him. She'd tried starting that life with the little bit of money they'd come into after his father had died. She'd found them a home in a respectable neighborhood, next to the best schools in the area. But then they'd lost that house because of poor money management (he still didn't know the ins and outs of all that had happened) and she'd dragged him in and out of homes in that same neighborhood, just about an hour away from Estes. She'd never been able to afford the sort of home she'd wanted and it had been that experience that had caused him to resent the real estate industry—not just the builders and contractors, but the agents, too.

He knew she would frown upon what he was doing...but he also knew she might find some skewed sense of justice to it.

Dougie came to the stairs and started descending. His steps were soft and a few seconds apart. His caution allowed him to hear the delicate footfalls from below. Soft, plotting...as if whoever was down there was also walking with caution, as if they, too, were try-ing to go unnoticed.

When he had only three steps left before he came to the first floor, Dougie stopped. He gripped the board tightly, its wooden surface digging into the flesh of his palm. He took a sudden step back when he realized that the late afternoon sunlight from the window above the front door had momentarily sketched his shadow along the floor.

He heard the footsteps drawing closer … closer.

He inhaled, held the breath, and waited.

And when he saw the woman come into view, he attacked.

Kate came to the rail where the steps started downstairs. She nearly started down them but then paused for a moment to stretch out her sore knee. She would not realize it until later, but it was likely that split second of self-care that saved her life.

The moment she stopped and extended her right leg out, she got the sense of something moving through the air. She looked up and, though it confused the hell out of her, her instincts caused her to jump back. Doing so with her leg outstretched resulted in her stumbling backward. As she did, she felt something—a piece of wood, from what she could tell—go sailing by her face. It missed her nose by less than three inches, and she could feel and smell the wood as it passed by. But it wasn't being thrown. No, it was being swung much like a baseball bat.

The adrenaline surging through her only briefly masked the pain in her knee. As she fell backward, her leg still outstretched, she stretched her knee out a bit *too* much. The pain was extraordi-nary. She screamed just as she saw the man who had been wielding the piece of lumber. He came bounding down the last few steps, already bringing the piece of wood back for another swing. As he did so, Kate's mind fired off what seemed like a billion thoughts, all one right behind the other.

This is the killer.

That piece of lumber is what he's been hitting the people with before hanging them.

And oh God, there's a rope in his other hand.

Kate fumbled for her gun, momentarily blinded by panic and the pain in her right knee. She unclasped the holster and had her hand on the grip but by the time she was able to actually start pulling it free, the man was bringing the wood down and hard across in an arc. Kate rolled hard to the right, barely avoiding the blow. The edge of the wood clipped her shoulder, but just barely.

She tried scrambling to her feet but in doing so, too much pressure was applied to her knee. She bellowed in pain as the knee buckled and gave out beneath her. Her back was to the killer, so she knew her only option at this point was to draw her gun, roll over, and hope she could draw on him before he smashed her face in with his wooden weapon.

But as it turned out, she did not have time for that. As she tried to roll over, she felt something slide over her head. It went over easily, almost naturally. And once it was over her head, she felt the smooth yet textured surface of the rope as it was pulled tight around her neck.

She pulled her gun but as she freed it, her hand was slapped away. She held on to the gun a moment longer but the pressure at her neck and her knee were too much to bear. If she didn't relieve some of the weight from her knee, she was afraid she might pass out from the pain. She tried scooting up on her left leg and as she did, the killer planted a knee hard into her back. The impact of it caused her to drop her Glock. It clattered uselessly to the floor, but she barely noticed it. She was too focused on the tightness around her neck and the feeling of being pulled backward.

She tried scrambling for purchase, but the wood floors were too slick. She did her best to keep her thoughts oriented, to keep herself from falling into panic. She relied on a tactic that had saved her life at least twice in the past—a tactic that attackers rarely even considered.

Rather than grasping for the portion of the rope that had been tied around her neck, Kate reached up over her head, trying to find the strand that she was being pulled by. She slapped at it, finally found a grip, and clutched it with both hands. She then planted her left foot against the edge of the bottom step (another stretch that was almost too much for her) and then pulled forward with all of her strength.

The killer had clearly not been expecting this. He came scrambling forward, colliding with Kate's back. Kate took advantage of this, reaching up and grabbing his head between her shoulder and forearm. She then fell to her back, as flat as she could, rolling to her side and applying a sloppy choke hold.

Her Glock was lying less than three feet away. She could reach for it, but doing so would free the killer. He was slapping at her blindly, his hands striking the side of her face, her chest, her shoulder. Her grip on him was weak and she knew he would be able to escape the hold in just several seconds. Given that, she supposed going for the gun was the wisest option.

She released him and then reached for the gun. Her fingers fell on it just as she was yanked backward. Apparently, the killer had never lost his hold in the rope. He held her away from the gun like a man walking a dog and pulling back on the leash. Kate gagged a bit, still reaching for the gun.

The killer then gave a violent tug of the rope. It was hard enough to make Kate lose any hope of regaining her feet. She went falling back to the floor, then sliding along it. She watched her Glock grow further and further away as she was choked and pulled backward at the same time.

She watched the world go sliding by as she grabbed for anything that might stop her. The rail for the downstairs steps went by, too high for her to grab. She tried rolling over to hook her left foot on that first stair going down but it was a clumsy effort that did nothing more than irritate her still-howling right knee.

She then saw the chandelier come into view. Made of iron and hovering about fifteen feet overhead, it looked like some weird spaceship. She recalled the victims from the other homes, hanging in some form or another, and knew what was coming. She had to do something, even if it meant injuring herself further. It was either suffering an injury or suffering a gruesome death.

Wincing at the pain she knew was coming, she planted her right foot on the floor, then her left. She scrambled behind the killer now, not being pulled anymore, but led. When she got to both of her feet, she launched off at him.

Pain exploded in her right knee. She screamed as she went into the killer in a tackle. It was well-aimed but not quite strong enough. She collided with him, only causing him to stumble backward a bit. She went for his wrist, trying to capture it between her hands. If she could just break his wrist, making it impossible for him to hold the damned rope...

But he yanked his hands away. He then brought his right hand back, still holding the board, and brought it down. Kate slipped to the left, dodging the blow, and managed to trap his arm between her own left arm and her side. She took the moment to her advantage, positioning her right hand palm-up and sending a driving punch into the killer's chin.

There was a loud *clink* as his teeth clamped together. The man's eyes went wide as he stumbled backward. She prayed the blow was enough to knock him out, but he managed to blink the attack away.

In his surprise, though, he had dropped the rope.

Kate dashed for the Glock. When she was close enough to it, almost back to the stairs, she dove for it, intending to slide.

But again, her damned knee slowed her down. Rather than sliding for the gun, it was more like a clumsy collapse. And as she reached for it, a clubbing blow fell along her back. She screamed out, curling into a slight ball to try her best to protect herself from the next blow from the chunk of wood.

But the killer had apparently had enough. He pulled the rope even tighter around her neck. Kate felt her eyes bulging and realized with dawning horror that with his new cinching, she could no longer draw breath in through her nose. She could manage a few shallow breaths through her mouth, but it was not nearly enough.

The killer pulled the rope even tighter and pulled her back toward the chandelier. Kate did her best to fight but as she rose up her knees, her right knee buckled again and the pain in her back from the blow was just too much. Her body tried to fall over but was held up by the taut rope. As it kept her from falling, it also strangled her.

Kate resorted to desperate measures, digging her fingers into the rope at her neck. She tried slipping her fingers between the rope and her skin, but it was just too tight. And with this realization, there came another: she could now no longer draw in *any* breath.

She gazed up at the killer. He was smiling, his brow starting to break out in sweat. Kate watched as he tossed the other end of the rope up over the chandelier. He did it with expert precision, as if he had been practicing the move for a while.

With the free end up and over the center of the chandelier, the killer gave another tug on Kate's end of the rope. It felt like it was slicing into her skin now, not only strangling her but cutting her open.

Little white spots started to flicker in her field of vision. She gasped, trying to scream, trying to do anything to free herself. But then the killer was pulling again. This time, he was grunting as some of Kate's weight came up off of the floor. She gagged against the motion, the top half of her body leaning forward. Those white flecks became red and black as her lungs started to beg for air.

The killer gave another pull. Kate felt her body trying to moan, to scream, to even simply grunt.

But it could no nothing. It was helpless now as this pull brought her to her feet and then, as if she had already left her own body, off of the floor.

CHAPTER TWENTY FIVE

She blacked out for a moment.

She was only aware of this because when the killer gave another violent pull on the rope, the jerking motion at her neck jarred her back to consciousness. Right away, she started gasping for breath. Her lungs were begging for air and her head was starting to ache. As she ran out of oxygen, she was surprised to find that her head was just as agonizing as her lungs; it felt as if there was pressure growing inside of her skull and that it might pop like a grape at any moment.

Her instinct told her to fight. Fight or flight had come and gone and now there was nothing but the primitive human need to survive. And while that panic-laced instinct was indeed front and center, the trained agent still operated somewhere distant, far behind the scenes.

This part of her was aware of two bits of information. It tried focusing on these tidbits, doing everything it could to keep Kate anchored to logic and strategy.

The first thing was that dust, plaster, and other bits of debris were gently raining down on her. She did not have to crane her neck upward (surely that would have been next to impossible as she dangled in the air) to know this was coming from the ceiling, where the base of the massive chandelier was being worked loose from the excessive weight being applied to it.

The second was that with the last pull of the rope, he had stepped closer to her. She didn't think it was arrogance on his part, but just a lack of awareness. She could easily regain control of her flailing legs and deliver a kick that would land squarely on his fore-head. But even then, there was no guarantee that he would drop the rope.

And given the tight, constricted feel of her lungs and the red tinges to everything in her field of vision, she figured she might have about five seconds before she passed out—and maybe never opened her eyes again.

Using this as fuel, Kate centered all of her fleeting strength to her core. She tightened her ab muscles and brought her legs up toward the killer. He saw it, assumed she was trying to kick out, and sidestepped her easily. This actually played to Kate's advantage, though. She rested her left leg on his shoulder, hooking her knee along the side of his neck. As he tried pulling to the right to escape this weak hold, she cradled the other side of her head with her right leg.

She felt instant relief against her neck and was suddenly able to draw in a series of small breaths as she now had weight beneath her to push off from. The killer tried fighting against her, but she had already started to wrap her calves around the front of his neck. She knew it must look ridiculous, this bastardized version of a tri-angle choke, but it was working. And surprisingly, the rope that was connecting them was making it more effective than she could have hoped; when he tried pulling away, it only tightened the pressure she applied to his neck.

And just like that, the tables had turned. Now *he* was the one fighting for breath. And if he continued to try pulling away, he was going to pull her with him, eventually tearing the chandelier from the ceiling.

Little by little, the breaths Kate was now able to draw in were larger. There were still spots in her vision, but her lungs were start-ing to feel normal again, her chest loosening up as she started to breathe more normally. She figured if she could maintain this hold for another thirty seconds or so, the killer would start to weaken considerably. And if he dropped the rope, she'd be freed. If he would—

Suddenly, the killer stopped fighting against her. Still holding the rope in his right hand, he grabbed her lower legs, trying to loosen the hold. When he realized she had it locked it tight, he started hammering away at her legs. He wasn't able to get much power behind the punches, as he was having to punch in a backward motion, but the panic and fury in them still made them quite effective.

Kate felt and heard a slightly primal growl escape from her throat as she clenched the sloppy triangle choke tighter. When she did, her right knee reminded her in drastic fashion that it had been hurt. Putting so much force on it sent a shuddering pain through her entire leg, one that resonated all the way up to her stomach.

The killer, sensing some sort of hesitation, continued to pummel her. The punching didn't do too much damage—until his right fist landed squarely on the side of her right knee.

The pain was immense. Her body reflexively released the hold and the killer was able to get out easily. He was sneering in anger, wasting no time when he stepped free. He grabbed the rope with both hands and gave it a hard tug. Kate felt herself launched upward, the pressure once again tight around her neck. Her legs kicked blindly, but the killer had distanced himself this time, having learned his lesson.

He circled around her, taking the free end of the rope to the stairs. There, he started to tie the rope around the railing. Kate looked from him to the floor beneath her, estimating that there was about five feet of open space between her floating feet and the hardwood floor.

The only thing she could think to do was to reach up for the rope that connected her neck to the chandelier. She figured if she could grab it and pull hard enough, maybe she could pull the chandelier right out of the ceiling. She reached up to do that but found it much harder than she had imagined. It was almost impossible to bend her body that way and even when she did manage to do it, she found that the rope was too far beyond her reach to do anything.

Again, her lungs started to ache, begging for air. Her neck felt like it was being crushed. And in a moment of absolute sadness, she thought of Melissa and Michelle. She thought of Allen. She thought of them getting the news that she had been killed—fifty-six years old and strung up from a rope while she'd been out acting like a thirty-year-old federal agent.

She let out a desperate little mewling noise, knowing that she was out of options … knowing this was how she was going to die.

Her legs started spasming as her body fought for oxygen. The edges of her vision were growing red, then black. Her head felt as if it were slowly floating off of her body and—

The world exploded. Or at least, that's what it sounded like. An exploding sort of sound, and the musical noise of broken glass, somewhere far off…

And then Kate was falling. She fell to the hardwood floor, striking her right knee yet again. The pain rocketed through her like a surge of electricity, and it was likely what kept her from blacking out.

Through foggy vision, she saw the murky shape of Agent DeMarco getting to her feet. Kate's sludgy mind put the scene together as well as she could. DeMarco had come in through the sliding glass doors on the back deck, somehow shattering them and spilling into the house. She was currently tacking the killer down, both of them sliding through little fragments of glass.

Kate rolled over onto her side, using her left leg to push herself back against the wall. Gasping and coughing, she watched as DeMarco did her best to pin the killer to the floor. She had a good hold on him but the glass was causing them to slip around more than the hardwood floors would have allowed.

DeMarco drove a hard elbow into the man's solar plexus and he screamed in what sounded like nothing more than a raspy puff of air. DeMarco used this moment to grab the man's left arm, tossing him over onto his stomach.

As he rolled, Kate saw the man's hand reach out, grabbing the plank of wood he had barely brained her with. She opened her mouth to shout a warning but her voice would not cooperate. Her neck was too sore, her windpipe aching from the rope which, she realized, was still wrapped around her neck.

As it turned out, DeMarco saw what he was reaching for. She reached out to stop him from grabbing it, but was a millisecond too late. By the time she was leaning forward to stop his arm, the killer brought the piece of wood up. It struck DeMarco in the side of the head—not too hard, but hard enough to knock her off of him.

He scrambled to his feet, took in the situation, and realized it might be best to just tuck his tail between his legs and retreat. He started for the door as DeMarco groggily picked herself up off of the floor. Kate looked to her right, saw her Glock still lying on the floor, and reached for it. She was still so weak that when she held out her arm, she nearly fell over on her right side. She grabbed the gun and brought it up just as the killer was unlocking the front door.

Kate pulled the trigger just as the killer opened the door and dashed out of it. The bullet that chipped the door frame was less than two inches from taking the killer right between the shoulder blades.

Kate's instincts took over and, without thinking, she got to her feet. When weight was put on her right leg, she fell against the wall. DeMarco was on her feet now, rushing for the front door.

"You hurt?" she asked.

"My damned knee," she managed to croak. Though, as she spoke, she wondered if there might also be something wrong with her throat now, too. Carefully, she removed the rope from around her neck. It was pulled right by the other end, still on the railing, but she managed to slip it off.

DeMarco nodded, satisfied that her partner was not near death, and hurried through the door after the killer. Kate hobbled to the door, too. Her right leg was now pretty much useless, so she could only lean against the doorway and watch as the killer hurried across the front yard, out toward the street. DeMarco was giving chase, but the killer had a good head start and looked to be very fast.

Kate figured DeMarco was so involved in the chase that she could not see the chain of events unfolding before them. From where she stood at the opened front door, Kate saw a car coming down Duffey Street. It was coming fast, but not really speeding. Still, unless the driver was paying very close attention, Kate was fairly certain of what was going to happen next.

Standing at the doorway, she tried screaming out again but it only pained her. The words came out, but they were little more than a whisper.

The killer glanced back to see how much of a lead he had on DeMarco. He did this just as he dashed out into the street. He did not turn back around until he heard the screeching of brakes. But by then, it was too late.

The car—a newer model Lexus—came to an abrupt stop but not before striking the killer. The corner of the hood caught him in the legs. The killer did a little half flip up onto the hood, bounced once, and then fell to the road in a heap. Kate doubted the impact had been enough to kill him, but it had sure as hell slowed him down.

DeMarco took immediate advantage, rounding the corner and falling on the man. The car hid what happened next, but Kate figured DeMarco must be putting handcuffs on the killer. Slowly, Kate lowered herself to the floor and scooted herself out onto the porch. As she reached into her pocket to notify Armstrong of all that had happened, she watched as the driver of the Lexus stepped out.

It was Brett Towers. He had the look of a man who had stepped out of a particularly surreal dream. He looked to the front of his car, rushing around to the side to where DeMarco was still busy with the killer.

Kate pulled up Armstrong's number and placed the call, not realizing until the phone started ringing that she was going to have to actually speak.

"This is Armstrong," the sheriff answered.

"Got him. On Duffey Street. It's not Redman ..."

She set her phone down, ending the call. Kate leaned against the door frame and did her best not to cry. In the thirty-four years of her career with the bureau, she had come close to being killed only once before. This had certainly been even closer than that, and it made her realize that perhaps she was indeed too old to keep up.

Her knee flared in pain, pulsing in a sick rhythm, as if to remind her of this.

She looked out to the street where Brett Towers got on his phone and placed a call. He was pacing back and forth, only stopping once to look at the damage the killer had done to the front right corner of his hood. Behind him, DeMarco finally got the killer to his feet, pressing him against the car. As she watched it all go down, she noticed something else.

Sitting half a block down the street, barely visible from the front door of the house, was the old worn-down black Taurus she had approached yesterday before becoming distracted by Regina Voss.

She had a very strong feeling that they would easily discover that it belonged to the man currently pressed against Brett Towers's car. The same man she had stood in front of and spoken to for a space of twenty seconds or so the day before.

It made Kate feel weary and almost sick. He'd been right there, right in front of her, and she hadn't known…

It was information she would likely be getting from a hospital room, as she was now convinced that her knee was in much worse shape than she had originally assumed. It continued to throb as she looked out to DeMarco, putting the finishing touches on the first case she had ever led.

CHAPTER TWENTY SIX

It had taken a lot of convincing, but DeMarco managed to get Kate into a wheelchair when they arrived at the hospital. DeMarco seemed more than happy to push Kate around the hospital while a small team of doctors escorted the killer to a private area to tend to his injuries. As it turned out, the car had caused more damage than Kate had assumed. The killer had at least a few broken ribs and a concussion. It could be worse, which was why the doctors were so quick to treat him.

"And now," DeMarco said as she wheeled Kate into the second floor waiting area, "we need to get you some attention."

"I'm fine for now. Just need some pain meds or something."

"I call bullshit."

A doctor came rushing up behind DeMarco, having branched off from the group that was tending to the killer. "I agree," she said. She was a younger woman, eyeing Kate with some odd blend of respect and sympathy. "If not for the knee, then the abrasions on your neck."

"I want to know about the killer first," Kate said.

"I'll update you as information comes in," DeMarco said. "Now for once, Kate...forget being Superwoman. Get yourself taken care of."

Kate said nothing, but was willing to admit defeat. She had been whooped pretty good; her neck felt like someone had taken a razor to it, her throat felt as if it had been crushed, and she didn't even want to speculate on just how badly she had screwed up her knee.

The doctor—who introduced herself as Dr. Kelley while pushing Kate to an examination room—was pleasant enough. She asked no questions about the case, or about how she had managed to hold her own. Instead, she remained quiet aside from the introductions...which Kate appreciated greatly.

As she was wheeled into an examination room, Kate pulled out her phone and noticed she had received a text. It had arrived while she was struggling with the killer. She opened up her text messages. When she saw that the text was from Allen, she almost felt guilty— almost like she did not deserve a man so loving and understanding.

Hope all is well. Sorry things got heated last time we talked. I miss you. I love you. Take care of yourself.

Something in her heart wanted to call him right then and there, to tell him what had happened to her. She was perfectly okay with being alone in these situations but in that moment, she would have given anything for him to be there while Dr. Kelley prepped the room and started asking her questions about the injury.

She answered the questions as well as she could, recounting the first time she had injured the area when she had hyperextended it during a foot chase almost twenty years ago. It felt like she was telling a story about someone else, some other woman she had heard about but had never met. It was not only surreal, but it was another reminder of how this part of her life could have easily closed a few years ago.

"Agent Wise?"

Kate realized that she had zoned out, staring at the wall across the room. She looked to Dr. Kelley and saw that she was offering Kate a small plastic cup with two pills inside.

"For the pain," Dr. Kelley said. "One will push it off a bit. Two will make you feel a little loopy."

Kate didn't think twice about taking them both. She did so with the small cup of water that Dr. Kelley also offered her.

"Okay, now," Dr. Kelley said. "We know the knee is going to need some attention. But let me get a look at that neck while I wait for the specialist to get in. With all due respect, it looks like you've been put through the wringer."

Kate offered a wry smile but only out of courtesy. She just wanted the day to be over. She just wanted the pills to kick in so the pain would stop and, hopefully, she could get that blank kind of rest that only really good pain relievers could provide.

"Kate?"

Kate stirred at the sound of her name. She knew the voice uttering it well. She opened her eyes and saw DeMarco sitting by the side of her hospital bed. "DeMarco...why are you still here?"

"Oh, it's only eight o'clock. You've been sleeping for about an hour and a half. I thought you might want the few updates we have on the killer."

"Yeah, thanks," Kate said. She was still groggy but did her best to break through it.

"His name is Dougie Hanks. He's thirty-one years old and grew up in New Castle. He worked at a furniture outlet in New Castle until recently. His mom passed away not too long ago and from what we can tell, he quit his job soon after."

"Moved to Estes?" Kate asked.

"We don't know. He has no permanent address in the town, though we have confirmation that he sort of bounced around a few hotels in the area. I'd assume if he was the one that had been squatting in those houses, that's where he was sleeping."

"Any idea how long?"

"No. And we're not being allowed to speak to him just yet."

"What about me?" Kate asked with a weary smile. "I think I sort of drifted off before Dr. Kelley could fill me in."

"Severe bruising to your neck and trachea but none of the abrasions were bad enough that they needed stitches. They lathered you up in antibiotic ointment and put on some bandages. Doesn't look

too bad. But the knee...they don't know yet. They have you scheduled for an MRI in about two hours."

Kate nodded, doing her best not to assume the worst. The painkillers had done their job, but she could still tell there was something clearly wrong with her knee. Somewhere very deep inside of
her, she was aware that some part of her heart *wanted* the injury to
be serious. Maybe then the constant back and forth of family and
finally letting her career go would be much easier.

"I'm worried about you, Kate."

It was a sweet sentiment, but Kate wasn't sure how to feel about
it. She couldn't help but feel a little embarrassed. She had been
assigned to assist DeMarco with the case and, she thought, had
helped in that regard. But she'd also managed to nearly get killed
in the process, left to watch DeMarco arrest the killer while she had
remained on the front porch with a busted knee.

Sounds sort of like a curtain call to me, she thought.

"There's nothing to worry about," Kate finally said. "I just need
to realize that I'm not young enough to ... well, to *anything.* You did
a good job on this one, DeMarco. Sorry I caused some drama there
at the end."

"Drama? Kate ... I was perfectly content to leave that arrest hanging on Matt Redman. It was *you* that had the second thought...the
thought to check that house. And lo and behold, you found the
killer."

"Oh gosh," Kate said. "What about the press conference?"

"Currently taking place. It got postponed when we found out
Redman wasn't our man. Sheriff Armstrong and her force have it
under wraps. I'm on call if she should need anything else."

"Thanks for saving my life," Kate said with a smile.

"Of course. And hey...dangerous or not, busting through that
sliding glass door was pretty awesome. Even got a few nicks and
cuts for my efforts." She showed Kate her right arm, which was ban-
daged up to cover the cuts.

"One more question, before I slip back into la-la land...what
made you decide to come?"

DeMarco smiled, but Kate could tell that it was a genuine one rather than the playful ones she often used to keep a situation feeling light. "Because I've come to trust your instincts. And when you texted me to fill me in, I knew. I knew we had the wrong guy and you were on to something."

That means a lot, Kate thought.

But the thought was never voiced. She could only smile back before the drugs pulled her back under.

CHAPTER TWENTY SEVEN

He remembered. Very big house—one so big that even as a kid, he knew his mother would never be able to afford it. They'd had to pass on so many houses due to what his mother called "financial hardships" that by the time he was thirteen, Dougie had been able to tell when a house was out of his mother's price range.

That one house, though … there had been a bedroom upstairs that he thought would be great for him. There was a walk-in closet with an attached attic. He'd imagined the little hiding spots and adventures he'd be able to experience if he managed to get that room. The bedroom window had looked out over a big backyard. In a neighboring yard, he'd seen two kids playing basketball and thought that could be him—out there playing basketball with some new friends.

But they had not gotten that house. They'd ended up living in an absolute shithole that his aunt had sold to his mother at an affordable price. His mother had said they'd been happy there, but he had never felt it. He wasn't sure why, but her simple love had never been enough. Shopping all those houses in those great neighborhoods, he'd felt like he'd missed something. And on some dark Saturday night when he figured he should have probably been out dating, he'd heard his mother crying. Her crying and the feeling that she had never been able to give him the life he had deserved had always killed him, but it got worse as he got older.

One night, sometime just before high school had let out, he'd dreamed of one of the real estate agents that had showed his mother those houses... the house with cool bedroom with the attached attic, as a matter of fact.

"No," he said out loud to the hospital room. "Can't think about that."

He'd done some bad things. Some very bad things. He wasn't sure if there was a God and, if there was, if that God would forgive him for all he'd done. He knew he didn't deserve it. And really, as he lay in that hospital bed, doped up on painkillers with four broken ribs, a separated shoulder, and a concussion, he could barely remember any of it. He remembered *enjoying* it, but he couldn't even remember the women's faces or why he'd hated them so badly.

"Guard?"

Just one word, but it sounded like he was weeping. Slowly, the tall black man who had been stationed outside of his door came into the room. He looked down at Dougie like he wanted to pull out his sidearm and blow his head off.

"What?" the policeman barked.

Dougie then asked the man a question. It was apparently not a question the policeman had been expecting because he asked to hear it again. Then he chuckled and left the room, and as far as Dougie was concerned, that was likely the end of it.

But although it was nearing eleven o'clock, he also felt the night was still young.

The good news was that it was not an ACL tear. The bad news was that she was still probably going to need surgery anyway. Kate found out at 11:37 that night that she had torn her meniscus and severely hyperextended her knee. By the time she was back in her room and Dr. Kelley had come by for her final rounds, Kate was starting to feel the painkillers wearing off.

"Two more," Dr. Kelley said, handing her a cup. "But try to wait another hour or so."

"Thanks," Kate said, taking them and wanting to pop at least one right away. The pain was coming back with force now, probably aggravated by the gentle yet insistent movements of the X-ray techs.

"What have you decided about surgery? Want us to do it here?"

"I'd prefer to be back in Richmond," she said. "No offense to you, of course."

"That's fine. So long as you can have your partner sign off on the responsibility of getting you back home as soon and as safely as possible."

"I understand."

"Well, Agent Wise, it was great to meet you. I'll have your X-rays and notes sent to the hospital in Richmond. I don't want you waiting too long, so I'd like for you to be on the road to get it taken care of by tomorrow. We'll brace you up in the morning after you've rested and the folks in Richmond can do the rest."

It sounded fine to Kate, though she was aware that the trip from Delaware to Richmond was going to be torment. But she wanted to see Allen. She wanted him there with her as she made it through the pain and the surgery.

With Dr. Kelley gone, Kate lay there, looking at the ceiling and doing her best to wait for the hour to pass so she could take the two new pills. She thought about calling Allen to let him know what had happened but didn't want to worry him. It would be best to do that face to face.

By the time she had talked herself out of calling him, there was a knock at the door. She looked up and saw DeMarco peeking in. "You awake?"

"Yeah...the pain is starting to fuss at me."

"Sorry to hear that," DeMarco said. "I'm also sorry to come by with this bit of news, but I figured you'd want to at least know."

"What is it?"

"Dougie Hanks is talking and coherent. He asked his guard if he could speak with us. I checked with the doctor and he said it should be fine...but that we shouldn't push on him too hard."

"He *asked* to speak with us?" Kate asked, wanting to make sure the pain and the remnants of the drugs hadn't made her hear DeMarco incorrectly.

"That's how I understand it."

"Then let's go."

"Kate, are you sure? I know you're in a lot of pain, and the doctor said you are going to need surg—"

"We'll make it quick," Kate said. "Help me into the wheelchair, will you?"

DeMarco did as she was asked. Kate felt she did a pretty heroic job of pretending the movement didn't hurt too badly. She had to bite in one little moan but was pleased to find that once she was sitting and her right leg was elevated, the pain subsided a bit. DeMarco rolled her down the hall and then to an elevator, which they took up two floors. Neither woman spoke a word during the walk to Dougie Hanks's room. When the guard saw them approaching, he gave a nod of acknowledgment before opening the door for them.

When Kate saw Dougie Hanks, she was alarmed at how mortified he looked. She did not think he was scared of them, but what he had tried to do to them. There was regret in his eyes, the sort of look she expected to see on the face of a driver who had accidentally run over some little girl's puppy in the middle of a highway.

"Thank you for coming," he said.

"Mr. Hanks, please spare us," DeMarco said. "My partner is in a great deal of pain—partly thanks to you—and I'd like to get her back to her room as quickly as possible. The only reason we're here is because she has one of the kindest hearts I've ever had the pleasure of experiencing."

"Yes... of course..."

"Five minutes," Kate said. She found it hard to look away from him. She tried to find any trace of the anger and borderline psychopathic delight she had seen in his eyes while they had fought in the house, but she could see none.

"I just wanted to apologize," Dougie said. "I... well, I knew what I was doing. I did for the other three women, too. I knew what I was doing and I planned it all out. But looking back on it now, I can barely remember it."

"Are you going to tell me it's like you weren't even there?" Kate asked. "I've heard that one before, Mr. Hanks. A few times, actually. And I've only ever seen it work in court a single time. So if you're going to try that…"

"No, no. I suppose if this goes to court, I won't deny it. I know I left things behind this time. The rope…the wood. Probably enough to pin me down. And I…well, I think I'm fine with that. With the other women, though…I could not apologize. But I can now. I can to you."

"And why should you apologize for something you barely remember?"

"Because you had nothing to do with why I did these things. I did it because of my mother and the way she was treated. Skewed justice or something. I don't know. But it made me feel good when I did it. I guess that means something is wrong with me, but that's fine. I think I've always known. But my mother would be ashamed of me. I know that now, but I lost sight of it when I was…when I was doing it. I did it for my mother, but she'd be ashamed of me."

Kate nodded. She had been in this situation before but in this particular moment, she was much more vulnerable that she had been in the past. Sometimes a murderer would seek forgiveness from a would-be victim because they feared what was to come—be it the legal system or the afterlife. But Dougie Hanks seemed legitimate. Now that he had been caught and could only face the realities of what he had done, the weight of it all seemed to be crushing him. Kate thought she could see it in his eyes and the way his frail body slouched in the hospital bed.

"What happened to your mother?" Kate asked. She genuinely wanted to know. She thought idly of the book she wanted to write, of how she had always, at the end of the day, sought to understand the reasons people chose to murder.

"It's a boring story and—though I am very sorry about what I tried to do to you—it's none of your business. But I'll just say that there were money issues after my father died. Mom wanted the best for me, and that included a nice, safe home. She became obsessed with getting us into a good home but she could never afford it and ... and that's all I'm going to say about that."

"Kate, come on," DeMarco whispered. "This is enough."

Kate nodded and said, "I don't accept your apology, Mr. Hanks. Maybe year ago, I would have but I'm old enough now to appreciate every year I have left. Every day. And you nearly took all of that from me. You *have* taken it from at least three women. So, no ... I don't accept." She wanted to say much more, to lay into him in a way she might regret later. But she knew that would only be the pain talking. Instead, she ended with saying: "DeMarco, let's go."

Again, DeMarco did as she was asked and backed Kate out of the room. Kate had no idea why she felt the need to cry, but it was there. She looked down to the little cup of pills she had been holding the entire time and tossed them back into her mouth. She swallowed them right now, along with the urge to weep.

There was no fanfare or big send-off when DeMarco and Kate left the hospital. When DeMarco stopped back by the Estes police station, there was very little fuss made. The parking lot was packed with traffic—including a few news vans—as DeMarco parked behind the building, out of sight from any prying eyes and cameras. She left Kate in the back seat, leg stretched out, as she went in to finalize some paperwork and to call Duran to fill him in on everything.

When someone tapped at the window a few moments later Kate was nearly completely dozed out by the tide of the most recent round of painkillers. Through hazy eyes, she saw that it was Armstrong. When Armstrong realized that Kate recognized her, she opened the driver's side door and peeked her head in.

"I just wanted to thank you for your help," Armstrong said. "And I'm so sorry about your leg. DeMarco said it wasn't as bad as it could have been, though. So I guess that's good."

"It is," Kate agreed. "But at my age, any injury like this could be the last injury, you know?"

"Is there anything I can do for you?" Armstrong asked.

Kate shook her head. "You're doing a good job here," she said. "Even DeMarco and I almost made the mistake of assuming Redman was the killer."

"But in the end, *you* knew better."

Kate knew it was meant as a compliment, but something about it did not sit well with her. *You knew better...*

She supposed some of it came from guilt. She had known better, all right... she had known better than to come rushing into this case, far too excited to prove herself after sitting on the sidelines for six weeks. She had known better than to once again place her job above Allen. But she had done both of those things.

And now she had a busted knee to show for it.

She meant to say *thanks*, but DeMarco was suddenly standing right there beside Armstrong. Kate was barely aware of the women talking as the tide of medicine came sweeping back in. Slowly, it started to take her over. She heard DeMarco talking to her, and then she was vaguely aware of the car moving.

Painkillers, the lull of an engine, and the movement of a well-tuned car all cradled her and pulled her into sleep. She dreamed distantly, like watching TV through someone else's window. In the dream she was in a poorly lit public park. Somewhere ahead of her, she knew her husband was about to be shot. She called Michael's name and tried to run after him, but her bum knee wouldn't let her.

She fell in the dream and heard the gunshot that had taken her husband's life.

And though she had no way of knowing it (and DeMarco certainly wasn't going to tell her), she moaned considerably in her sleep for the next fifteen minutes.

CHAPTER TWENTY EIGHT

Two weeks later, Kate's orthopedic doctor made the call that she was going to need surgery. There had been the smallest glimmer of hope that she might be able to heal without it, but two weeks following her exit from Estes, the only thing that had changed had been an increase in the amount of pain she was experiencing.

The prospect of surgery did not bother her. She'd had two surgeries over the course of her life—Melissa's C-section birth, and the removal of her wisdom teeth. No, what scared her was that she knew a surgery of this scope, at her age, might mean the end of many things.

As she lay in her hospital bed, waiting for the surgeon to come in to discuss, she recalled a moment back in Estes where she had actually hoped the knee was blown out because it would make the decision between a normal retired life and one last hoorah with her career an easy one. But now that she was faced with surgery on her right knee, that hope had become a reality and she was finding that she was not quite ready for the decision to be made for her after all.

Allen sat next to her, holding her hand and looking at her thoughtfully. Things were different for them now. The past two weeks had dealt them good and bad news alike. First, Allen's trip had gone well. After some basic paperwork and one last meeting, he'd be bringing home a very nice chunk of money and he would officially be retired by the end of the year. The bad news, of course, had been that Kate would indeed need surgery on her knee.

"When they take me back," Kate said, "I'd like for you to text Melissa."

"Of course."

Melissa had fallen into a new job in the past few weeks, one that looked to be very promising. She still had a few semesters of college to finish up and was finally coming to terms with the fact that she was just going to be one of those people who didn't graduate until they were twenty-six. Kate had been her cheerleader through it all, always brushing aside any mention of how she had graduated from college and then the academy by the time she was twenty-three.

God, that seems like a lifetime ago, Kate thought.

Before she could go down that rabbit hole, her doctor came in. He was a young man by the name of Dr. Foster. He ironically reminded Kate of Dr. Kelley. Looking at them, it was easy to think they might be brother and sister.

"So, it's time," Dr. Foster said. He was smiling, maybe a little too brightly. It made Kate think he knew something that she did not. "But before we take you back to get started, I'd like to speak with you in private."

Allen straightened up. "What for?"

Kate knew that sometimes, doctors asked female patients for a word in private, just to make sure things were good at home and that there would be a support system for them when they returned home. But she wasn't so sure that was why Dr. Foster wanted her alone. Still, she didn't want Allen to be alarmed either way.

"It's okay, Allen," she said. "It's standard for women patients."

Allen didn't look so certain, but he got up obediently. He kissed her on the forehead and walked toward the door. "I'll be in the waiting room," he said before closing the door.

When Allen was gone, Dr. Foster took a seat in the chair Allen had been occupying. He carried a clipboard in his hands but didn't look at it. Instead, he looked straight at Kate. It drove her nuts that she could not read his face.

"Is something wrong?" she asked.

"I really don't know how to answer that. You're perfectly healthy, Ms. Wise—with the exception of the knee, of course. And as far as I can tell, you're in such good shape that you should be able to recover from this surgery in no time."

"Do you think I'll be able to work anymore?"

Dr. Foster grinned here and shrugged. "Well, from what I understand, this last case had you tackling someone on a roof and being hung by your neck. I would never advise *anyone* to do any of that, much less a fifty-six-year-old woman. Now, I know it's poor taste to mention a woman's age, but for just a second, I think we need to dwell on that. You're fifty-six and are perfectly physically fit, bum knee aside. As a matter of fact, I'd feel comfortable saying there are probably some forty-year-olds out there that would kill to have your physique."

"With all due respect," Kate said, "I appreciate the compliments, but I know when someone is trying to sneak up to a point. So can we just get to it?"

"Agent Wise, we ran your blood work and the results came back about fifteen minutes ago. From what I'm seeing, you are somehow pregnant."

The words made no sense to her. She knew what they meant but it seemed as if someone had told her a joke and her brain was trying to figure out the punchline. When it all sorted itself out, only one word came to mind.

"Bullshit."

Foster smiled but got to his feet and showed her the test results. "When I saw it, I had them run the test again and it showed the same results. Obviously, we'd like to run an actual verified pregnancy test but I can tell you right now that when we catch it in a blood test, it turns out to be accurate more than ninety percent of the time."

"I'm fifty-six..."

"I know. I made a point to make a big deal about that a few seconds ago, remember?"

"How's that even possible?"

"It's uncommon for women your age to get pregnant, but not entirely unheard of. As a matter of fact, a friend of mine in this very hospital delivered a healthy baby boy to a forty-nine-year-old woman just a few weeks ago."

"I'm not forty-nine," Kate said, getting irritated and, if she was being honest, scared.

"I know. But yes…it is very uncommon, but it does happen. I'd have to check my facts on this, but there have been reports of women as old as sixty getting pregnant without any medical assistance. Again…it's uncommon, but it does happen."

"You'll forgive me if I don't feel super special and privileged."

"Well, I wanted to tell you by yourself. I see no ring on your finger, so can I assume the man that was here with you is a boyfriend?"

"He is."

"And would he be—?"

"Yes. If this insane news you're giving me right now is in fact true, he would be the father."

"Would you like for me to call him in? I thought you might want to know…and to maybe tell him before the surgery."

She thought about it for a moment and then shook her head. "No. Not yet. I don't even…I don't even know what I'm going to do about it."

"I understand. Want me to call him back in anyway? Just so you can process it all as we get ready for the surgery?"

"Yes, please."

Foster walked toward the door and paused, turning back to her. "Are you going to be okay, Agent Wise?"

"Yeah," she said, though the roulette wheel of emotions was still rolling in her head and she had no idea how to feel about what she had just heard. Part of her was still waiting for Foster to tell her he was just kidding, but when he closed the door behind him without saying anything else, she knew this wasn't going to happen.

"What the hell?" she said to the empty room. "What in the absolute *hell*?"

She remained in silence until Allen reentered the room three minutes later. He took his seat again, reaching out and taking her hand.

"Nervous?" he asked.

A little sob caught in her throat. She almost told him, but she could not seem to find the strength to gather those impossible words together.

I'm pregnant.

"No," she said, surprised to find that she meant it. "No, I'm not nervous at all."

With that, she smiled at him and suddenly had a pretty good idea of what she had to do—and what her life might look like from this point on.

Now Available for Pre-Order!

IF SHE HEARD
(A Kate Wise Mystery—Book 6)

"A masterpiece of thriller and mystery. Blake Pierce did a magnificent job developing characters with a psychological side so well described that we feel inside their minds, follow their fears and cheer for their success. Full of twists, this book will keep you awake until the turn of the last page."
—Books and Movie Reviews, Roberto Mattos (re Once Gone)

IF SHE HEARD (A Kate Wise Mystery) is book #7 in a new psychological thriller series by bestselling author Blake Pierce, whose #1 bestseller Once Gone (Book #1) (a free download) has received over 1,000 five star reviews.

Two teenagers, home for their winter break from college, are found murdered in their hometown. There is clearly a serial killer on a rampage, and the FBI is stumped—but can FBI agent Kate Wise, 55, still recovering from giving birth, enter his twisted mind and stop him before another girl dies?

An action-packed thriller with heart-pounding suspense, IF SHE HEARD is book #7 in a riveting new series that will leave you turning pages late into the night.

Book #8 in the KATE WISE MYSTERY SERIES will be available soon.

IF SHE HEARD
(A Kate Wise Mystery—Book 6)

Did you know that I've written multiple novels in the mystery genre? If you haven't read all my series, click the image below to download a series starter!

Made in the USA
Middletown, DE
25 January 2021